CW00766218

THE THEFT OF MAGNA CARTA

If someone were to ask you what was the most sacred,
most priceless relic of English history, you would probably
plump for Magna Carta, that repository of the ancient
liberties of this land. Suppose they then said: "Well, how
much will you give me for it?"
There are such people. And there are those who would buy,
even knowing that they could never show off their treasure.
Neil Stephenson and his beautiful 'wife' Sarah might just
have got away with it if a simple country copper (or
maybe not so simple) had not been suspicious of their
English contact man. The copper took a chance and,
without approval from his superiors, he telephoned West
at the Yard.
And so Chief Detective Superintendent West is drawn into
the situation, learning what he can from local lore experts
and his own contacts and helpers, and spotting one or two
things they miss . . .
Magna Carta *is* stolen . . . But that is not the end of the
story . . .

Other Inspector West books:

INSPECTOR WEST TAKES CHARGE
INSPECTOR WEST LEAVES TOWN
INSPECTOR WEST AT HOME
INSPECTOR WEST REGRETS
HOLIDAY FOR INSPECTOR WEST
TRIUMPH FOR INSPECTOR WEST
BATTLE FOR INSPECTOR WEST
INSPECTOR WEST KICKS OFF
INSPECTOR WEST CRIES WOLF
INSPECTOR WEST ALONE
PUZZLE FOR INSPECTOR WEST
A CASE FOR INSPECTOR WEST
INSPECTOR WEST AT BAY
SEND FOR INSPECTOR WEST
A GUN FOR INSPECTOR WEST
A BEAUTY FOR INSPECTOR WEST
INSPECTOR WEST MAKES HASTE
TWO FOR INSPECTOR WEST
A PRINCE FOR INSPECTOR WEST
PARCELS FOR INSPECTOR WEST
ACCIDENT FOR INSPECTOR WEST
FIND INSPECTOR WEST
STRIKE FOR DEATH
MURDER, LONDON-NEW YORK
DEATH OF A RACE HORSE
THE CASE OF THE INNOCENT VICTIMS
MURDER ON THE LINE
THE SCENE OF THE CRIME
DEATH IN COLD PRINT
POLICEMAN'S DREAD
HANG THE LITTLE MAN
LOOK THREE WAYS AT MURDER
MURDER, LONDON-AUSTRALIA
MURDER, LONDON-SOUTH AFRICA
THE EXECUTIONERS
SO YOUNG TO BURN
MURDER, LONDON-MIAMI
A PART FOR A POLICEMAN
ALIBI
A SPLINTER OF GLASS

The Theft of Magna Carta

The 41st story of Roger West

JOHN CREASEY

HODDER AND STOUGHTON
LONDON SYDNEY AUCKLAND TORONTO

Copyright © 1973 by John Creasey. First printed 1973. ISBN 0 340 16486 7. The characters in this book are entirely imaginary and bear no relation to any living person. All rights reserved. No part of this publication may be reproduced or transmitted in any form or by any means, electronic or mechanical, including photocopy, recording, or any information storage and retrieval system, without permission in writing from the publisher. Printed in Great Britain for Hodder and Stoughton Limited, St. Paul's House, Warwick Lane, London EC4P 4AH by The Garden City Press Limited, Letchworth, Hertfordshire SG6 1JS.

Author's Note

There are some inconsistencies and inaccuracies towards the end of this book, relating to the security arrangements at Salisbury cathedral and for Magna Carta as well as other priceless manuscripts. These discrepancies are quite deliberate, for I should hate to give any secrets away. One of the most heartening things I discovered in researching was how many security secrets exist. And I am sure that some were discreetly concealed from me.

As is my custom I wrote this book first out of remembered facts, for one is researching all the time and storing up much information — some of it false, faked or forgotten. After the first writing was done I went to the cathedral for help to get the facts right.

If at first I was regarded with mild suspicion when making inquiries, once it had been make clear that I really wasn't planning to steal the Sarum Magna Carta much careful and courteous help was given me.

I shall always be warmly grateful to them all.

JOHN CREASEY

Contents

I

The Temptation

"How MUCH IS IT WORTH?" Neil Stephenson asked.

"It is beyond price," answered Caldicott.

"Don't give me that," replied Stephenson. "Everything has its price, from the Koh-i-Nor diamond to virtue. How much is it worth?"

Caldicott paused for what seemed a long time.

He was with the American in a fifteenth-century inn which overlooked the Wiltshire Avon and, not far across the water meadows, the mass of grey stone which was Salisbury cathedral. It was early evening. They sat on green slatted chairs at a green-painted table ringed with the marks of many glasses and tankards of beer, as many glasses of wine. Behind them was the old, thatched inn with a new motel attached, and banks of flowers in bewildering and beautiful array. On one side, shining in golden glory on to the spire of the cathedral, the sun was still hours from its setting.

The evening was pleasantly warm. A breeze, off the river, was not strong enough to stir the grass or the leaves or the flowers, yet could be felt. The insects, all tiny, hovered in their secret flight, yet could be heard. Three swans, arching their necks with pretended indifference to a group of people watching them from the bank within the inn's meadow, looked as if they were made of millions of flakes of snow. Ducks in great variety, feathers green and blue and brown and grey, yellow and black and also white, gobbled at the low-flying insects; only one dived for whatever succulence was beneath the surface, its rear end poking towards the sky, and now and again disappearing only to bob up again.

Neil Stephenson was in his forties, sandy-haired, fresh-complexioned, with pale eyelashes and pale eyebrows; his face was a mass of liver-coloured freckles; so were his hands. Sitting, he looked squat because he was very broad. He wore a perfectly fitting, pale green jacket, and sand-to-yellow trousers. In front of him was a dry Martini, hardly touched although now and again he fingered the stem of the glass; whenever he did, sunlight shimmered on a gold ring on the third finger of his left hand.

Caldicott, Frank Caldicott, was English; brown tweed-clad; bushy brown-haired; bushy dark-eyebrowed. He had a heavy face and heavy jowl and a lugubrious expression. Curiously, his eyes were blue. In front of him was a whisky-and-soda, the bubbles still rising occasionally from the bottom and sides of a plain glass.

"Frank," Stephenson said, without impatience, "you don't often hesitate this long."

"I'm not hesitating," Caldicott replied.

"You haven't answered."

"I answered," Caldicott said.

"You didn't tell me how much it is worth."

"I told you it's beyond price," replied Caldicott, and he stared towards the cathedral and its noble spire. His gaze was not on the spire, however, but on a spot near a flying buttress above some saints which had escaped disfigurement or destruction when Cromwell sent his vengeful men against the churches which had been loyal to king as well as to creed.

This time, Stephenson did not give a glib reply, but watched Caldicott, whose eyes, caught aslanting by the sun, had not only a strange light but a strange intentness. More: they had a reflection of the spire and of a tree, between the bank and the cathedral; the tree had pale green leaves spread quite thin, so that it was like a veil between the inn and the church which was just two hundred years older.

"What are you looking at?" Stephenson asked. There seemed a touch of uneasiness in his voice, and he picked up his glass very quickly, and sipped the Martini in the manner of an abstemious man. "Anyone would think you could see through the wall."

Without taking his gaze away, without changing his expression, Caldicott picked up his whisky-and-soda, sipped, and said:

"In a way, I can."

"I don't understand you today," complained Stephenson. "Half the time you seem to be talking nonsense."

"No doubt," said Caldicott. "No doubt I do." There was a dreamy note in his voice. "I'm a romantic," he went on. "You didn't know that. I am a romantic and a dreamer, Neil. But you're not. You're a hard, practical realist, aren't you? You haven't a stick of humour in your make-up. You'd even take it seriously if I say I would like to jump into that river. I talk about a piece of history and you want to know how much it's worth."

"Why don't you?" asked Stephenson.

"Why don't I what?"

"Jump into the river," Stephenson said, glaring.

Caldicott seemed so taken aback that he gaped at the speckled face and the yellowish-green eyes. For a moment there was utter stillness and silence between them, until the tension seemed to twang. Two things broke it. One was a woman coming from the side of the motel. She picked her way down a narrow, winding path, through antirrhinum and phlox, polyanthus and bright blue forget-me-nots, a lilac bush and a patch of grass gay with buttercups and daisies. The other was Stephenson, bursting into a guffaw of laughter, slapping his knee, making everyone on the river bank look at him. Two ducks waddled in alarm towards the water; blackbirds and sparrows, starlings and martins flew away from the raucous noise.

"Haw-haw-haw!" roared Stephenson. "You thought I was serious, didn't you? You thought I wanted you to jump into the water!" He leaned farther back in his paroxysm of mirth, until suddenly his expression changed, alarm chased delight away, and he thrust himself forward as his chair began to topple backwards. He grabbed the table between thumb and fingers and slowly steadied himself. Safe, he gave another little cackle of laughter. "Didn't you?" He scrambled to his feet and saw that the black legs of the chair had sunk inches into rain-soaked turf. At the same time, he became aware of the woman, now on the grass and walking towards them.

She was small; not tiny, but small. She wore a loose-fitting suit of chain-knit, pearl-grey in colour. Her dark hair was beautifully groomed, almost as if she had come straight from a hairdresser. Her legs were exceptionally well-shaped and she walked with fawn-like delicacy. Her face had a mask-like quality, not from make-up, which was not overdone, but from the set of her looks and the blankness in eyes so grey that they were silvery, although the sun reflecting off the water touched them with gold.

Caldicott stood up, admiration plain in his expression.

"Hallo, Sarah," he said. "You're early."

"Hi, Sal," welcomed Stephenson. "Did you see me tip over?"

"You won't believe me," the woman said in a smooth voice, "but I even heard your shout of terror." She sat on a chair which Caldicott pushed into position for her, looking beyond both men to the cathedral; a glow began to soften her eyes.

"That wasn't a shout of terror," denied Stephenson, beaming. "I told Frankie to go jump in the river and he thought I meant it! *Ha-ha-ha!* Didn't you, Frankie?"

"I certainly did," Caldicott agreed solemnly. "What will you have to drink?" he asked Sarah. "I don't think there's any service out here but the bar's only a step away."

"When are we going to have dinner?" asked Sarah.

"Whenever you like."

"Then I'd like to sit here for five minutes and then go and eat," Sarah replied.

She eased her chair round; two of the feet had already gone half-an-inch into the soggy turf. She did not remark on how beautiful it was but looked from the cathedral to the trees, from trees to river and the birds, from river to the flowered terraces. Her eyes kindled, their expression gentle, as if she felt both calm and content. A child, unnoticed until then, suddenly ran from his parents towards the river, making a dozen ducks cackle in fright and waddle away, and the smaller birds fly. Only a few yards from the calm water, a young woman with long legs and a revealing mini ran with grace towards the child, while the man with her downed beer from a tankard and watched. The woman caught the toddler from behind and lifted him high; and the boy pointed to now distant birds and declared:

"Birds."

"That's right, birds," his mother echoed. She had a long, plain face but moved beautifully even when she shifted the child from one side to the other so that he could see the whole expanse of river and meadow. Now, she pointed: "Swan," she said as a swan, still outwardly indifferent to noise and people, floated by in a lordly manner.

"Swa'," the child mimicked.

The mother pointed again, and said: "Duck," as a duck, emboldened, climbed clumsily from the river to the grass.

" 'Uck," echoed the child.

Sarah watched the mother and child, Caldicott watched Sarah, Stephenson kept glancing towards the spot at which Caldicott had been looking before Sarah had joined them. It was he who broke the silence, and as he did so the mask fell over Sarah's face.

Does she hate him? Caldicott wondered. And he thought: She's a real beauty. I wonder how faithful she is to him.

Stephenson was saying: "Honey, would you believe there's a big pile of money in that cathedral? At least that's what Frankie says: a big pile of money."

"You said that?" Sarah asked, her voice tainted by a hint of disgust.

"No," answered Caldicott.

"Well, you implied —" Stephenson began.

"I told him that there was something in the cathedral that was beyond price," corrected Caldicott, talking the other down. "And from then on he couldn't stop trying to put a price on its vellum."

Sarah stared across the water.

"You mean, the copy of Magna Carta?"

"If copy is the word."

"It's my word."

"It just has to have a price," insisted Stephenson, and then he muttered under his breath: "Everything has." When neither of the others responded, he went on more loudly: "I don't understand Frankie tonight. He said he could see through walls."

"And the ages," declared Caldicott. "Centuries."

"I tell you, he's nuts!"

"What can you see, Frank?" Sarah asked, and her gaze rested on him for a moment, with a hint of a smile at her eyes and lips.

The mother and the father passed, the child between them, a hand in a hand of each of its parents. "'*Uck, S'an, bird,*" he was repeating. "'*Uck, s'an, bird.*" They passed between the table and the limpid river. A white-coated waiter appeared, and hovered; so there was service.

"Change your mind?" urged Caldicott.

"All right," Sarah said. "I'll have a tomato juice."

"Just a tomato juice? No gin, rum, vodka —"

"A plain tomato juice," insisted Sarah.

"A tomato juice," echoed the waiter. "With or without Worcester sauce, miss?"

"Without," said Sarah.

"Mine's a Martini," Stephenson said. "Make it very dry."

"With a twist of lemon, sir, or an onion?"

"Plain, not fancy," Stephenson growled.

"Nothing for me," Caldicott said; his glass was half-full, he sipped only a little whenever he raised it to his lips. "Will you ask the head waiter if we can have a window table? We'll be along in ten minutes or so."

"I'll see what I can do, sir," the waiter replied. "A table for how many, please?"

"The three of us."

"Thank you, sir."

Caldicott was only partly distracted by the man and his questions; he was much more concerned with Sarah. The way she held her head, tilted slightly backward, the curve of her throat, the shallow V of her blouse and the gentle swell beneath — my God! What a woman she was; and could be. He felt a stirring in his loins, rare for him unless he were alone and close with a woman, and then reminded himself that he was at least as intrigued by her reaction to the cathedral and her quiet: "You mean, the copy of Magna

Carta." As far as he knew she was as fresh to Salisbury as Stephenson, who hadn't the faintest idea what was here. She had known; she had a great deal of general knowledge and hid it behind that expression of inscrutability.

She looked back at him.

"Well, what can you see, Frank?"

Stephenson drained his glass, began to tip the chair back again and hurriedly righted it, then sat leaning forward on the table. He did not appear to be listening but Caldicott was quite sure that with his literal mind he took in everything that was said, the fanciful and the real. As he talked, Caldicott himself wondered what had stirred him. He was by reputation a taciturn or at best a matter-of-fact man.

"I can see the bishops and clergy, and the abbot supervising the building of the cathedral," he explained dreamily. "And the heavy stones being drawn by men with ropes on their shoulders. I can see the stone-masons and the labourers, the wood-workers and the painters, on the rough scaffolding. And I can see the little town, like a toy town, huddled close by. I can see pigs and hens and cattle grazing in the close, too. Have you seen the close?"

"What's a close?" asked Stephenson, perfunctorily.

"The area contained by the cathedral walls," Caldicott answered. Now the glow in his eyes had a dreamy quality. "And I can see the vellum in the cathedral library over there, one of the four remaining copies of Magna Carta left of twelve originals which were made of the document."

"Not copies," corrected Sarah. "Originals. There were twelve, and each one was inscribed separately." She smiled warmly at Caldicott. "Can you see the scribes working?"

"Yes," Caldicott said. "I can also see the barons at Runnymede, forcing John to sign each one!"

"Set his seal," Sarah corrected again. "There's a lot of argument as to whether he ever really signed any of the charters. *Is* a seal a signature?" she asked musingly.

"Say," interrupted Stephenson.

"Yes?" asked Caldicott, patiently.

"How many of these copies — okay, okay, versions — are there?"

"Originally there were twelve," Sarah repeated. "Today —"

"*Twelve!*" exclaimed Stephenson. "You mean to say they mass-produced this Magna Carta? What makes you think it's worth so much? Okay, okay, the one here is beyond price. If there were twelve —"

He seemed to become aware that both Caldicott and Sarah were staring at him in a curiously forbidding way, and he stopped talking and actually looked abashed as if he had become vicariously aware that his attitude was near-sacrilegious and a cause for shame. They were all silent for a long time, until suddenly Sarah put out a hand and patted the back of his. Hers was small and white and smoothly kept; the back of his was hairy and rough and the fingers short and stubby. His face lit up when she touched him, and on the instant a pang stabbed through Caldicott and, almost unbelieving, he recognised it for what it was: jealousy.

How big a fool could one be?

"Just take it from Frank and me," Sarah said. "That piece of vellum is beyond price."

"Okay, okay," replied Stephenson, without impatience or exasperation. "It's beyond price. But if it wasn't, if some guy was to go up to another guy, maybe old Nicodemus you hear so much about, how much could he get for that Magna Carta? I mean, are we talking in thousands or in millions? That's what I want to know."

His voice fell away. The others looked at each other, then averted their gaze. Caldicott had to grit his teeth to stop himself from laughing, and caught a glimpse of laughter in Sarah's eyes. Her lips moved. She asked a question in a voice so low-pitched that Caldicott had difficulty in hearing, but Stephenson heard clearly because her head was now turned towards him.

"Pounds?" she asked. "Or dollars?"

It was no use. Caldicott spluttered and began to laugh; and Sarah burst out laughing too. They were so convulsed that their chairs rocked, a little suck of sound coming each time a foot was pulled out of the rough turf. And as they laughed and Stephenson stared from one to the other,

* *

apparently too puzzled to be annoyed, the parents with their child passed again and the child, huge-eyed, stared, stopped, and announced:

"Man laughing."

"Lady laughing too," the mother managed to say, and she smiled at Caldicott, who could not see her clearly for his happy tears.

2

Sobersides

"ALL RIGHT," Neil Stephenson said, "I still don't know what was so funny."

"I'm not sure that I do, now," temporised Caldicott. "Can't we forget it?"

"*I* can't," stated Stephenson, flatly.

"Neil," said Sarah, putting her hand on his arm; this seemed to be a soothing gesture which never failed, "we weren't laughing at you, really. We just saw the funny side, and I caught Frank's eye."

"Oh, don't be silly," Stephenson said, patting her hand. "I'm not annoyed. I'm just puzzled. How you two can be so obtuse I don't know."

"Obtuse!" exclaimed Sarah.

"Us!" gasped Caldicott.

"Listen," said Stephenson with great earnestness, "you two think you're so clever and maybe in some ways you are, but in other ways you've got no sense at all." He gave Sarah's hand a little squeeze, then moved his arm away and picked up his brandy glass.

It was after ten o'clock that evening.

They had dined well in a full dining-room where there had been no chance to talk about anything confidential. They had talked about the cathedral and Salisbury and nearby Stonehenge, as well as about Magna Carta and the garbled history which they had acquired through hearsay and from small guide books. And they had talked of King John and the barons and their peers who had forced acceptance on him. Now they were in a corner of a bar which had a low ceiling, criss-crossed with dark oak beams; there were more beams in the wall. One end of the room was filled with bottles of all colours, standing in the recess of history. The trio had comfortable chairs, Sarah sitting between the two of them and being noticed by every man and most women who passed the open door or came into the bar. She had a dry ginger ale in front of her; the men, brandy in medium-sized bowl-shaped glasses.

Caldicott and Sarah were still reeling from Stephenson's: "You've got no sense at all." He did not appear to be amused or even smugly satisfied by his triumph, but went on in a tone of unfeigned exasperation: "Well, you haven't even seen the possibilities, have you?"

"*What* possibilities?" demanded Caldicott.

Neil Stephenson seemed to change in front of their eyes. The exasperation faded. An expression of intense concentration took over. His forehead furrowed and his lips tightened. He glanced across the room at three men at the bar and the woman behind it, listening to a conversation about farm prices and agricultural workers' wages. He glanced at the door, too, as he hitched his chair a little closer and lowered his voice so that only his companions could hear. His eyes lost their vagueness and glinted sharply.

"If it's as valuable as you say, old Nicodemus would find a market. We're here to look over those paintings at Leech's, but we don't have to do any more than look. We would find out the best way to get hold of that old parchment —"

Caldicott almost choked: "You mean, steal Magna Carta?"

"So you're beginning to see straight," Stephenson said. "That's exactly what I mean, Frankie. Steal that bit of parchment and *then* find out how much it's worth." He raised his head and gave a *tck-tck-tck-tck* of a laugh, an echo of his great guffaw. Looking from Sarah to Caldicott, he tried to choke back the sound, but his whole face was pinky-yellow and radiant. "Then we'd know what all the fuss is about, wouldn't we?" He almost spluttered, threw back his head again and gasped: "*Tck-tck-tck-tck*," and when he had recovered sufficiently he went on in a hoarse voice: "Now who's got no sense of humour?"

Sarah said: "It's impossible!"

"It would be as bad as sacrilege," declared Caldicott. "I wouldn't have anything to do with it."

"*Tck-tck*," went Stephenson. "I'll find out what old Nick would pay, and then we'll see how smug you are." He sat back and sniffed the brandy with unexpected delicacy, glancing from one to the other over the rim of the glass. "I know one thing," he went on. "It would have to be a quick job. A very quick job."

"I tell you it's impossible," insisted Sarah.

"I heard you the first time. I heard Frankie, too. It would be as bad as a sacrilege and he wouldn't have anything to do with it. *Tck-tck*."

He was still enjoying his joke when a man came in and, instead of going straight to the bar, approached their corner. He wore a corduroy suit of greeny-brown with big brass buttons and a tweed cap, both a little too small for him. His eyes were small and porcine, while his nose was broad at the bridge and nipped at the nostrils. The slightly odd appearance was heightened by a faint suggestion of a hare-lip. There was something both merry and earnest about him, and he appeared completely oblivious to the startled way in which they reacted to his approach.

"Good evening, one and all," he said in a rather broad accent; anyone locally would have recognised it as from north Wiltshire, with the long, slurred 'a' making all sound rather like 'arl' and the way he shortened 'good' to 'g'd'. "I hope you won't mind me interrupting, but I couldn't help hearing what you were talking about at dinner."

"At dinner!" exploded Caldicott.

"That's right, sir, at dinner," The 's' in 'sir' was nearly but not quite a 'z'. "About Magna Carta and the cathedral, and all that. I wondered how interested you were, because there are one or two little titbits of information I might be able to give you." Without waiting for an answer, but placing both hands on their small table and looking down at them, he contrived to indicate the three men at the bar. "You see that silvery-haired gentleman over there, now. John Withers, his name is. You'd never believe he lived in a house built on ground one of the Runnymede barons lived on, would you?" The newcomer eased his weight off the table impressively, and declared: "But it's a fact."

"You mean, one of the forty-eight barons," Sarah asked, incredulously.

"That's right," said their visitor. "You've done your homework, Miss, and no doubt about it. He lives at Bodenham, Newall Lodge, Bodenham, and that land was given by King John to Sir John Botenham — with a 't' — one of his cronies. Fascinating how we live right in the middle of history around these parts, isn't it?"

"Fascinating is the word," agreed Sarah, warmly.

"Is this Withers a descendant, or something?" asked Stephenson, obviously ready to be impressed.

"Lord love us, no, sir! He bought the place a few years ago, and converted it. Some people say it's vandalism but that old place was going to rack and ruin and he bought it and turned it into flats. Very nice ones, too. And the way he keeps the grounds is a real treat. I've a friend who lives there. They say he's always looking for old tiles and bits of pottery from the places where the workers camped when the cathedral was being built. No, the irony of it is that *King* John gave the land to *Sir* John, and then a few years afterwards *Sir* John was one of those barons who forced Magna Carta down *King* John's throat, as it were. If you see what I mean."

Sarah was smiling.

"I see exactly what you mean. It's very good of you to take the trouble to tell us."

"Think nothing of it," replied the stranger. "I like to pass on a little local folklore to visitors to Salisbury. Salisbury people are proud of their city, you know, and I'm Salisbury born and bred. Batten's my name. Tom Batten." He shook hands all round. "Well! Must be on my way, the missus doesn't like being left on her own on a Monday. Ah, and that reminds me, tomorrow's market day, it's an open market here and well worth a visit. Look out for the Batten family stall, my brothers are farmers, it has the best butter and cheese in the market, I'll swear to that."

As he broke off, the woman behind the bar called: "Last drinks, gentlemen, please."

"Now don't be worried, that doesn't apply to guests in the hotel, residents as they call 'em," Tom Batten reassured them. "You can drink as long as there's anyone up to serve you."

"Will you have a drink?" asked Stephenson.

"Bless you, no, I've had all I can carry tonight, and having to drive home in the bargain. I really must be getting along."

"Oh, come on," Stephenson urged. "Why don't we go and join your friends at the bar." He stood up, almost dragging Sarah with him.

The man Batten's protestations died away.

At close quarters, Withers proved to have a very clear, unlined face and laughing blue-grey eyes. He was too plump, and seemed very warm. The other man with him was a smaller, clean-shaven type, with very dark eyes and dark, clipped sideburns. He was introduced as Jacob Leech.

"Gee, that's quite a coincidence," Stephenson declared. "I've come to see some pictures at a Leech Gallery tomorrow. An auction preview. Ain't it a small world. Is the name Leech very common around here?"

"Not very," answered Leech. "I'm the owner of the gallery."

"Well, what do you know! It's like having a preview of a preview!" Stephenson, suddenly boisterous and excited, ordered drinks for them all, and then hurled question after question at Leech about his pre-auction viewing. Leech parried skilfully, Withers watched with apparent amusement and made an occasional comment, while Caldicott and Sarah stayed on the fringe of the discussion. They did not say much to each other but Caldicott's eyes seldom shifted their gaze from her face. Some women would have found this almost embarrassing but Sarah seemed oblivious, and was certainly not put out.

The woman at the bar said: "You really must drink up, gentlemen."

"You never said a truer word," Tom Batten agreed. He thrust a hand into his trouser pocket and drew out a ring of keys. "Is there anything I can help you people with in the morning? Any place you'd really like to see?" His eyes brightened. "Have you seen Stonehenge, now, that's only a few miles away?"

"No, thank you," Stephenson said. "We're just passing through, and going straight on, after the preview."

"That's right," Caldicott nodded. "But you're very kind."

"Always glad to help strangers to get to know Salisbury," Batten assured him, and backed away. "It's been a pleasure talking to you folks." He smiled, somehow making his nose wrinkle and giving his whole face a porcine expression, and turned away. At the same time he waved his keys at the little group in the corner, and called:

"Goodnight, Lucy, goodnight all."

" 'Night, Tom."

"See you tomorrow, Tom," Withers said.

"That I will," Tom Batten replied, and went out.

"Now I must be on my way," Leech said.

"So must I," declared Withers, shaking hands. "I'll look forward to seeing you at the preview."

"Sure will," enthused Stephenson. "I sure will."

Stephenson watched until they were out of sight, then sniffed the bouquet and drank his brandy down. "Nice people," he remarked, and glanced across at the bar, as if deciding whether to have another brandy. Sarah put her hand lightly on his, and said: "Time we went to bed, Neil." She stood up and waited for Neil to get up, then hesitated and asked: "Would you like a stroll by the river?"

"This late?" Stephenson sounded shocked. "No, sir! Ma'am!" He placed both hands on the arm of his chair and hoisted himself to his feet.

Sarah led the way out, and up the narrow oak staircase, with wall beams and cross beams. On the wall on one side were some old farm implements, and several iron traps, including a huge man-trap; all were freshly painted black. She called "Goodnight" and Stephenson grunted to Caldicott as he followed.

A porter was coming along the narrow passage which connected the fifteenth-century part of the inn, the original Rose and Briar, with its newly-built motel section.

"How late are these doors open?" Caldicott asked.

"Oh, they'll be open for at least another hour, sir."

"Good," Caldicott said, and went out into a yard which led to the meadow and the riverside. As he came within sight of the starlit sky and the reflection of the stars and of lights from the inn on the water, he ran his hand across his forehead. It struck chill out here, yet he felt warm. He actually shivered as he walked over the heavy turf. A couple stood in shadows, hugging; kissing. A sound of radio or television music came from one of the rooms; a car passed in the road beyond the inn itself.

Caldicott shivered again. He was soon able to discern the tables and chairs, and the now glossy-looking surface of the river. Behind him, lights at several of the motel apartments were on but all the curtains were drawn. Across the river he could just make out the tall cathedral spire, partly because of the red light at the very top, a warning to aircraft in bad weather. Caldicott moved away, towards the motel. Sarah must have come that way deliberately, this evening, to walk through the garden. Now she was in one of the rooms, a back room he knew, overlooking the garden and the river.

That was all he knew.

He had come from London to meet Stephenson and Sarah and go with them to examine the collection of paintings at one of the city's many antique stores, where the paintings were on view prior to auction at a larger hotel in the city. There were rumours that Leech had uncovered a rare collection of Old Masters at a farmhouse between Salisbury and Wilton; rumours that there were at least a dozen eighteenth-century masterpieces, with two Constables, a Gainsborough and two Stubbs and a Turner. Caldicott was an expert on paintings, a first-class judge of values, and Stephenson was one of the biggest buyers of stolen paintings and works of art in the United States. His great strength, as a receiver, was that he carried in his mind a long list of buyers willing to purchase stolen property; men who would buy works of art for their private collections which were never shown to the world. Such collectors would derive enough satisfaction simply from possession of a masterpiece. The fact that they could never show other people what they possessed was not important.

Caldicott had been asked to come to advise Stephenson

on the value of these particular paintings. They had done business together often before, in London, in the United States, in Paris, Madrid, Milan and Rome, as well as the Scandinavian countries; and they did business by letter and by telegram.

They had arranged to meet in Salisbury because the Stephensons had wanted to come a day ahead of the preview.

Caldicott, a widower of long standing, had never met Sarah Stephenson before; had not in fact known of her existence. He had seen her for the first time here at the Rose and Briar; and he had never been more affected by a woman. Now, as he strolled through the garden, he could not get the thought of her out of his mind. What on earth was such a beauty doing married to a moron like Stephenson? It was repellent: why wasn't *she* repelled by the man? How could she bear to touch him as she did, with a familiarity which seemed to be born of affection?

She had suggested a walk in the grounds. He had fooled himself into thinking that if he came out here, she would eventually appear, but she did not. The couple who had kissed and hugged for so long, left the spot arm in arm. Some cars left and others arrived. The porter appeared, visiting all the tables; and as he collected empty glasses and coffee cups, he said to Caldicott:

"We'll be locking up in a few minutes, sir, now."

"I'll be there very soon," Caldicott promised.

He scanned the windows again, wondering which was Sarah's, longing to see her. Even when he reached his own room and told himself he was behaving like a fool, he could not get her out of his mind. She was at once the most composed, poised and beautiful woman he had ever met.

And married to that humourless idiot!

At last, he went to bed, half-dreaming over her; and at last he fell asleep. The remarkable thing was that he had become so infatuated that he had quite forgotten Stephenson's ludicrous proposal to find out how much some collector of secret treasures would pay for the Salisbury Magna Carta. Another thing, nearly as remarkable, was that he had not given the man Batten, Tom Batten, another thought, categorising him as a local zealot with a loquacious habit and a good heart.

Certainly it did not occur to him that Detective Sergeant Thomas Batten of the Wiltshire Constabulary had recognised him, although Batten had not the slightest idea who the Stephensons were.

3

Roger West

CHIEF SUPERINTENDENT ROGER WEST of New Scotland
Yard had friends and acquaintances in many parts of
England; in fact, many parts of the world. There were those
whom he had visited on assignments; there were as many
who had come to the Yard and worked with him there. One
of the vital requisites of a police officer, of course, was to
remember not only names and faces but to fit them to
places and events. Deep in his mind was a kind of photograph
album of people whom he could identify after a few
moments. He had often reflected that his own 'album' was
not a variation of a Rogues' Gallery; there was little or no
need to remember criminals, for their records were on tap
at the Yard. Moreover the new system at the Scotland Yard
on Broadway, London, S.W.1 was remarkably efficient. One
pressed a button for a dossier on a man and, seven-and-a-half
minutes later a file virtually fell into one's hands.

He had never ceased to marvel at the conveyor belt in
its near perpetual motion on the seventh floor of the new
building. Like a great many senior officers who had known
the old building on the Embankment near Westminster
Bridge for his whole working career, he had lacked enthu-
siasm for the new, modern premises. But he had soon come
to admit that what it lacked in the picturesque it made up
for in efficiency. He was never likely to feel that it was
'home'; but it was now a kind of home from home.

On the morning which followed the meeting of the
Stephensons and Caldicott at the Rose and Briar in Salisbury,

he did a rare thing: walked from his home in Chelsea to the Yard, having left his car at the garage there the day before. It took an hour, and before he was halfway there he began to wonder about his wisdom, but on the whole he was glad.

He was on his own at home during that particular week, and nothing prevented him from getting a light breakfast and starting off early: in fact at a quarter to eight. Much of the previous evening he had spent virtuously mowing his front lawn and weeding the flower patches. His was a pleasant house in a pleasant street of houses built between the wars. Most of the other owners were enthusiastic gardeners. The spring flower season was over; most of the flowering trees and shrubs were gone, but a few late lilacs were in bloom, and some late may — it had been a long cold winter — and antirrhinums were abundant if rather leggy. He had two round beds of violets of which he was especially proud, and some beds of forget-me-nots. A perfume of flowers wafted as he walked past his own garden and that of his neighbours. King's Road, hardly a thoroughfare of great aesthetic beauty, had a rare freshness this morning, and every antique dealer appeared to have cleaned his showrooms.

Can't imagine how so many of them keep going, he mused, passing a row of three such shops and an art gallery in one short block. But he did not dwell for long on art or antiques. Instead, he reflected on his own life, his career and his future. Only a few weeks before he had rejected an offer from one of the private security companies to join them, but sooner or later he might have to accept such an offer.

A tall, powerful man in his late forties, looking no more than forty-one or two because of his fair hair, unlined face and brisk walk, he was 'old' as age went at the Yard these days. Long gone was the time when he was 'the youngest Chief Inspector' and later the youngest Superintendent on the Metropolitan Police Force. Thirty-five was 'old' these days; many men younger than he were retiring to civil jobs. Now that he was having a week of looking after himself, his wife being away with family friends and his two sons being out of London, he had plenty of time to ponder and reflect; it was no longer necessary to do everything under pressure.

When he reached the Yard he turned into the Victoria Street entrance, which was almost deserted, and went up in the nearer lifts. This, the highest building in the complex, housed the Criminal Investigation Department. He walked along plain, bare-walled passages past a succession of doors, and turned into his own office. It was small but compact, with a window overlooking the complex 'well' and his large desk stood in front of the longer wall, half-hidden by the door before one was right inside the room. A small pile of reports stood on the desk but his 'Out' and his 'Pending' filing trays were empty. For some inexplicable reason he was in the middle of a run of easy-to-solve cases; clues and evidence all fitted in quickly. As a result desk work had fallen off and pressures at the Yard had slackened more than he could remember. When this trend had first revealed itself he had suspected that hierarchy, including the Commander C.I.D., Coppell, was diverting work from him. But it wasn't that. Early summer had brought a lull which was continuing.

Instead of being grateful and taking the chance to slacken off, he had become almost fretful; at times there was hardly enough to do. And this would happen when Janet was away!

He sat down, opened the file, read a typewritten note saying: *The Commander would like to see you in his office at ten o'clock,* wondered why, and was interrupted by the telephone. He picked up the instrument mechanically.

"West."

"Good morning, Mr. West," a man said in a voice he recognised as from the west of England. "You won't remember me, I'm afraid — my name is Batten, Tom Batten of Salisbury."

Small, deepset eyes; distended nostrils; an odd-shaped face in every way, just a little like the pigs for which Wiltshire was famous, came at once to Roger's mind, and with it the lonely farm in the Avon Valley which had been burned to the ground, three bodies with it. He had gone down to help the Wiltshire Police with inquiries which had lasted over a month.

"Indeed I do," Roger said mildly. "Your wife cooks the best game pie I've ever tasted."

"So you do remember!" Batten was obviously delighted. "I said to Florence only half-an-hour ago that you have a better memory than any man I've ever met. Mr. West, I don't want to take up a lot of your time and I may be on a wild-goose chase, but I ran into a man last night I recognised, and if I'm right I would like to know what he's up to in Salisbury."

"Who is he?" asked Roger.

"A man named Caldicott, Frank Caldicott," answered Batten. "I thought I would check if you know anything about him. He's registered in that name at a local pub. He's a valuer of paintings and fine art, if I remember rightly —"

"And you're the man who's talking about my memory!" exclaimed Roger. "Give me twenty minutes, and I'll call you back."

"Very kind of you," said Batten. "The number's Salisbury 7654 — extension 17."

After he had hung up the receiver, Roger made a note of the number. He was nearly sure that Caldicott was out and about; someone had mentioned him lately: ah! Kempton, one of the younger men who specialised in fine art. Before asking *Records* it might be a good idea to call Kempton. He dialled the other's number, and Kempton answered at once.

"Chief Inspector Kempton."

"Superintendent West."

"Good morning, sir!" The formality between ranks was as rigid as ever, new building or not.

"What can you tell me of a man named Caldicott — Frank Caldicott?" asked Roger.

"I can tell you he's one of the most slippery customers I've ever had to deal with," answered Kempton, on the instant. "I'm pretty sure he's been on the fringe of a lot of art thefts but I've never found anything to prove it. I suspect he's a kind of high-class runner, if you know what I mean."

"Tell me," invited Roger.

"Very well, sir. As you well know, the art trade has hundreds of runners who go from shop to shop, reporting what one place has just bought and what's generally available.

A gallery might have a customer for a painting in the Reynolds School, say, and he'll pay a runner to find what there is about. And the system's much more widespread than it used to be. Runners used to cover only London and the big cities, but nowadays they cover small towns and villages too. Small dealers you've never heard of get on the list of some of the big boys. It's a curious thing in a way how much valuable stuff there is in the country. Half the dealers don't know the value of their stocks especially if they buy it up cheap — sorry, sir!" exclaimed Kempton, and there was a rueful laugh in a voice which had already become near-breathless; when Roger didn't speak, he went on in a self-chastened mood: "I get carried away on this business. I —" He paused and then blurted out: "I wonder if you could spare me an hour some time."

"Yes," Roger said. He vacillated between saying there was no time like the present, and the wisdom of taking his time; he decided not to rush it. "I'll be in touch soon. Meanwhile, this man Caldicott."

"The simple answer is that he's a very shrewd judge and he's often been seen at showrooms and galleries, even private houses, a week or two before a robbery. But he always appears to be in the clear, doesn't seem to have anything at all to do with the actual job. What's your interest in him, may I ask?"

"He's down at Salisbury, and a Salisbury C.I.D. man recognised him."

"That sounds in character," Kempton answered. "That stuff at Leech's Gallery, I suppose." So he kept his finger on the pulse in the provinces as well as London. "He goes everywhere — never know where he'll turn up next. If anything develops will you let me know, sir?"

"Yes," Roger answered, and rang off.

He pushed his chair back and pondered. Clearly, Kempton was a zealot, and the Yard couldn't do without some. He, Roger, hadn't worked with him a great deal and their last meeting had been a brief one in the canteen. And he, Roger, hadn't realised that Kempton had been concentrating on art thefts. It was surprising how departmentalised one could get, so to speak — be aware of one's own and any major job but be virtually oblivious of what was going on in the rest of the C.I.D. He put in a call to Salisbury and ran through the rest of the papers on his desk. They nearly all covered jobs which were at trial stage. Perhaps Coppell wanted to see him about an assignment: there was nothing he would like more.

His bell rang.

"You've been very quick, Mr. West," Batten said.

"I found the man who could give me the information we needed off the cuff," said Roger. "Caldicott has never been in jail but he's known to be very knowledgeable and at least one of our chaps is suspicious of him."

"*That's* a relief," Batten said. "I'd persuaded my C.I. to detail an officer to watch him, and this fully justifies it."

"Good," Roger said. "Will you let us know what happens?"

"I certainly will, Mr. West. We've had so many art thefts in this area lately, including the one at Longford Castle, I don't want anyone to slip through my fingers. Goodbye, sir, and thank you again."

Roger, replacing the receiver, wondered whether there could be more to Batten's calls than he had admitted: that last remark seemed to have widened the issues a great deal. Roger tucked this fact into the back of his mind, then picked up the newspapers. There was little or nothing of interest: Great Scott, he was actually waiting for ten o'clock! At least he could go and eat in the canteen, toast and coffee didn't satisfy him for long. What he needed, he decided, was to plan a few days ahead carefully. A morning with *Fingerprints*, for instance, another with *Records*; one with *Photography* and another with *Ballistics*. In other words, take some refresher courses. It was easy to allow developments in detective sciences and medical jurisprudence to get past one. The danger was that he should take his knowledge of the different departments for granted.

Should he make out a schedule? If he did he must use it casually, the 'just dropping in' technique. He moved from his office to another, reached by a communicating door. The room was shared by two detective sergeants and two detective officers who worked for him and the Superintendent whose office was directly opposite his.

"I'll be in the canteen, Venables," he said to a very tall, youthful but ungainly looking man nearest him.

"Very good, sir. You won't forget the Commander, will you?"

"No," Roger promised.

"Thank you, sir."

He was formal, everyone was formal, but then they always were. Why was it getting on his nerves this morning? It wasn't simply because of Coppell; he had felt restless from the time he had got up. The number of 'Good morning, sirs' seemed ludicrous as he walked along to the lift. When it arrived, there were five men and a youngish woman in it, all of subordinate rank. The 'Good morning, sir' was like a celestial chorus. Roger went into the canteen, headed for the nearly empty cafeteria and took some bacon, eggs and a sausage on his plate and carried it, with coffee, to an empty table. Across the room was Coppell, with one of the other Commanders, and as Roger glanced over a tall, attractive-looking woman, the Commander of the Women's Branch, joined the two senior men.

Was it his imagination? Or were they nodding and looking towards him?

It was five minutes to ten when Roger left, without having said a word to anybody; this was his morning for communing with himself. Coppell had gone, the other Commanders were still there. At ten o'clock on the stroke he tapped at Coppell's door. A man, replacement for a once sour-faced and hostile woman secretary, called come in as he got to his feet.

"Good morning, sir."

"Good morning."

"The Commander said would you go straight in."

Roger tapped gladly on a communicating door and went inside.

Coppell was a big, very thickset man: oxlike at the shoulders and heavy, bovine of feature. They had never been particularly friendly, and in fact had been hostile on occasions but they had come to respect each other. Nevertheless, Roger was seldom wholly at ease with the man, who usually gave the impression that he had something disagreeable to say even if he didn't say it.

"Good morning, sir," Roger said; and was sharply conscious that Coppell must have heard this a dozen times already.

Coppell grunted: "Sit down." He made a half-gesture with his right hand, enough to draw attention to it and to the thick, rather leathery-looking fingers. At the same time he studied Roger with eyes which were only half-open. A sense of foreboding strengthened in Roger's mind: he had the strong feeling that if Coppell had anything disagreeable to say this was a morning when it would come out. A dozen times at least Roger had entered this office aware of some reason why Coppell should be antagonistic; he knew of none this morning.

Abruptly, Coppell asked: "Ever seriously think of retiring, West?"

Roger was so taken aback that he didn't answer at once. Coppell's shrewd eyes were on him, he knew from experience that the other often sensed his thoughts; and too often guessed wrong. Now he sat solid and silent.

Roger answered: "Yes. Whenever I have, I've decided not to."

"I know of at least one time when you could have made a packet if you had," Coppell remarked. "Had any more offers from the private security firms?"

"I've had some feelers, but no more direct offers," Roger replied.

"Been tempted?" demanded Coppell.

There was something in his mind that Roger couldn't fathom, but one fear began to grow until it made his heart thump: that Coppell might be saying, in a roundabout and heavy-handed way, that it was time he did resign: take a job with Allsafe, or Securitor or one of the provincial firms which concentrated mostly on industrial crimes, largely spying. There was just one thing to remember about Coppell: he was very bad at dissembling, he liked everything straight from the shoulder or not at all.

"Not since the Allsafe job," he said.

"Wife more settled?" demanded Coppell.

What the devil had Janet to do with this? And what the devil was Coppell driving at? He hadn't once shifted in his chair since Roger had sat down.

"On the whole, yes," Roger answered. "She —" He broke off.

"Go on," urged Coppell.

"She has had a lot of problems to cope with, including the fact that both boys are away a great deal. Martin is planning to emigrate to Australia and Richard has a job with G.A. Television which takes him away a great deal. But —" He broke off, hesitated, then squared his shoulders and asked bluntly: "But what's all this about, sir? What has my wife got to do with it? Why do you want to know if I'm thinking of retiring?" When Coppell didn't answer at once he went on gruffly: "Is that what you want me to do?"

There was absolutely no way of telling from Coppell's expression whether he had hit the nail on the head.

4

Good and Bad

COPPELL WAS SILENT for so long that Roger's heart hammered as it hadn't for a long time. From the room next door came the faint tap-tap-tap-tap of a typewriter being used at great speed. Roger leaned back in his chair, now nearly convinced that he was right and that they were going to ask him to retire. The first and most vital thing was that he must take the blow well. If the ultimatum came then he would have to face it, but he must not show Coppell how much he hated the very thought: how much the idea hurt.

Coppell said: "No. No, it isn't."

Roger's heart gave a wild leap and settled very slowly. He relaxed as slowly. He was not aware of the beading of perspiration on his forehead and upper lip, or of the fact that he gradually changed colour, betraying his feelings more in relief than he had under tension. At last Coppell shifted in his chair, sitting upright, placing both sets of fingers on the edge of his desk.

"But —" he began, and gulped.

What the hell is he playing at? Roger wondered; but he did not go tense again.

"There are problems," went on Coppell. "Of promotion."

"Promotion," Roger echoed.

"That's right. No prospects."

Roger said hesitantly: "I don't quite understand you. No prospects of what?"

"Don't be a bloody fool," Coppell burst out. "Can only mean one thing. There are no prospects of promotion for you, Handsome." Good God, *he* was under strain at least as much as Roger! "Dead end. And you're not a dead end man."

"Oh," Roger said, and then weakly: "No." He had not grasped the full significance of what Coppell had said, and that was his, Roger's, fault: it could not have been put more plainly. But — why put it at all? He slipped his right hand to his jacket pocket to a silver cigarette case which he seldom used.

"Smoke if you want to," Coppell said. "I've cut out cigarettes, cigars in the evening is my limit now." He watched Roger light up while he went on in a voice which was much easier if a little hoarse. "The fact is, I hope to be going in the next six months. I recommended you for the next in succession but the proposal was turned down." Roger felt a sudden dowsing of spirits. "General feeling is that we've had too many short-term Commanders in the past few years. Each man puts a stamp on the job. I was only a stand-in, you know that as well as I do, lasted longer than I expected." Coppell gave a fleeting grin. "The V.I.P.s — and this includes the Home Secretary and the permanent secretaries there — all agree that we want to establish a team of Commanders for each of the departments, deputies, the lot, at a fairly young age level. Forty or thereabouts. There's going to be a concentrated effort to increase efficiency — prevention at least as much as detection — and the team selected has to be one which can and will stick together for a longish period. Ten years or more." Coppell drew a deep breath. "Rules you out."

"Yes," Roger admitted. "But it's a damned good plan."

"Think so?" Coppell was obviously relieved at this reaction.

"I don't see how we can get better results if we don't have something like this," Roger went on. He had steadied completely and was quite calm. More, he felt more warmly than he had even done towards Coppell, who had obviously hated the job of giving him this news. It was pretty clear now what was to follow: they wouldn't make him retire, they simply pointed out the disadvantages of not staying in the Force. He felt a warmth ooze from him, he was sweating again, but there was no tension, rather, a kind of hollow feeling.

"Good," Coppell said, enthusiastically. "Glad that's what you feel. Well now, cards on the table. We — I'm speaking for the Commissioners, A.C.s. and Commanders, we met yesterday afternoon — thought you should know this, and also that if you decide to take an outside job, no one would blame you. You could get a ten-year contract at three times the money you're getting here if you went now, and you would be released. See?"

"Clearly," Roger said.

"That's why I tried to find out whether you want to go."

Roger didn't answer.

"Let's have it straight," Coppell said, more aggressive than he had been since this interview had started. "I got the idea you don't want to go. That retirement is anathema to you. Right?"

Roger drew a deep breath.

"Right."

"That's what I wanted to hear," declared Coppell, with sudden, unexpected warmth. "That's what the doctor ordered! I stuck my neck out, too. I said this was how you would respond. All the same — think about it. Have to put yourself first in these things, you know. No one else can lead your life for you." He was speaking very quickly, as if getting through something that had to be said as quickly as he could. "Can they?"

"No," Roger agreed, and went on gruffly: "Supposing you give it to me straight, sir. What are you covering up?"

"Covering up my foot," growled Coppell. "Covering nothing. The point is, you're one of the most experienced men in the Force. Got a better record of cases solved than anyone else. There are only three other senior officers here who have your kind of general experience and you have one thing the others haven't got. A wider range of contacts. Do you know you've been to more foreign countries on assignment than anyone else on the Force? America half-a-dozen times, Australia, South Africa, nearly every country in Europe — you name it, you've worked with the Forces in those places and always done a damned good job." As Roger began to sway under this unexpected praise, Coppell gave a sudden, lopsided grin, and went on: "Can't understand it. Always rubbed me up the wrong way but you've got on with everyone else. White, black, yellow or what-have-you. I must have brought the worst out in you."

Roger didn't speak until it was obvious that Coppell was waiting for comment; so he said: "Well, something's bringing the best out of you now!"

"That's enough, that's enough," growled Coppell. "Truth is, whether I want to admit it or not, you've got a better record in what you could call public relationship than anyone. Even have the Press eating out of your hand half the time. And what the Yard needs is two things, Handsome. Your experience and knowledge *and* your ability to get on with people. So we don't want you to go."

"Good God!" exclaimed Roger.

"Surprise, surprise," Coppell retorted gruffly. "It's a fact. I've authority to tell you that if you'll stay in your present rank for another six years, then you'll be given a supplementary rank which hasn't been named yet, carrying a twenty per cent rise in income. Which is pretty well Commander's pay. I don't know whether they will really give you a fancy title, I do know they'll want to call on your general knowledge and experience and that thing you've got they call a flair. They want to cash in on you, that's the truth of it. You've always been known as the glamour boy of the Yard and they want to use you to improve the Yard's image while *they* improve performance. Not that performance is so bad. Well!" Coppell leaned back, huge against the back of his chair. "How does it sound, Handsome?"

Roger West sat upright, looked at Coppell steadily, raised both hands from the arms of his chair and dropped them again. He started to speak, couldn't find words, raised and dropped his hands again, and then said gruffly:

"The stuff that dreams are made of."

"Handsome," Coppell said, coming forward and stretching out his hand, "I'm bloody glad. I really am. I'm bloody glad."

His hand crushed Roger's.

The odd thing was that Roger simply couldn't speak. And he didn't as he moved towards the door, Coppell ushering him out, a gratified Coppell whose opinion was vindicated, who in his peculiar way was as eager to put the Yard before his own interests as Roger was.

"As soon as it's been made official you can tell the world," Coppell said. "For the time being, keep it to yourself, Handsome."

"Of course," Roger said. "Of course."

He went out.

He did not go to his office but down in the lift to the ground floor. He went out into the bright sunlight of Victoria Street and crossed to the other side, then took the side streets towards the river. At first he could hardly believe that what he had heard was true; could hardly take it in. If he had ever dreamed of a job it was something like this: he had not envisaged anything as good, nothing like as gratifying, but he had always hankered after a job which was a kind of roving commission. Once or twice it crossed his mind that in a way the Powers That Be were taking him off routine work and giving him a consolation prize, but it wasn't that. Others had been virtually compelled to retire at forty-five, one or two even earlier. This wasn't a sop to his pride, this was a job the Yard needed done.

He reached the river opposite the great new commercial buildings. The Thames had never looked brighter, the pleasure boats were gay, the barges solid and purposeful. He drank in the view, the sunlight and the news which Coppell had given him. If there was a flaw it was that he couldn't tell a soul yet; not even Janet.

But wouldn't she be in the seventh heaven when she was home and he could tell her!

When he turned away from the river, a cab was approaching, its *For Hire* sign up. He hailed it, got in, said: "New Scotland Yard," and was startled when the driver said: "Right away, Mr. West." And a moment later, through the open section of the partition, he wanted to know: "Caught any good crooks lately?"

Roger grinned.

And then he threw back his head and roared with laughter.

When he reached the Yard again he was still in a mood for laughter. This mood of elation wouldn't last, of course, his spirits were bound to droop, but he would always have the sense of deep satisfaction that he had now. The job would need defining, but that wasn't important: what mattered was that his future was settled in a way that could not reasonably be bettered.

At last, he was back in his office.

It was nearly twelve o'clock, nearly time for lunch! *Lunch.* He looked through his files, but no messages of any consequence had come in. There was his own note, to call and talk to Kempton. Was this the right occasion? He decided that it wasn't: his mood of elation would reveal itself too clearly. What he needed was a good, solid job to get his teeth into; it was time he came out of the clouds.

His external telephone bell rang.

"West," he said, as he picked it up.

"Oh, Mr. West." It was Batten from Salisbury in his unmistakable voice. "I'm sorry to worry you again but I *am* rather concerned about this man Caldicott. I haven't asked my chief, Inspector Isherwood, if we can call in the Yard yet, in fact there's nothing officially we could ask you to come for, but — well, I wouldn't be too surprised if Caldicott hasn't been down here to set up an art theft. An officer I think I told you about is taking some photographs of him and a man and woman who were with him last night and this morning. She's at the Leech Gallery now. It's a very good one, and the owner and an assistant go round the sales — auctions and private sales — in the area, and they have very good judgment; by provincial standards, of course. I had a word with Jacob Leech and he thinks he's made a big discovery: some Old Masters bought from a local farmhouse — gentleman-farmer kind of place. If he's right he's got a Gainsborough, two Constables and a Watteau. Now what would this Caldicott and his friends be doing there, do you think?"

Almost without a pause, Roger answered: "Valuing the pictures."

"Or identifying them," responded Batten. "Same thing

really." He seemed to gulp before going on: "Mr. West, it has to be unofficial, well, at best semi-official, but could you arrange for a Yard expert to come and see these pictures? This afternoon, I mean. If they *are* what Leech thinks then we ought to place a special guard on that shop tonight, but I don't think my chief would agree unless he had more than guess-work to go on. And that's all I have, really, isn't it?"

Roger said: "I see what you mean."

He needed that job to get his teeth into, but couldn't pose as an expert in old paintings or fine art. Yet Batten was obviously concerned, not without reason; Caldicott's interest in the paintings could indeed mean that a theft was being planned. He, Roger, wanted to talk to Kempton, and unless Kempton were on a job he couldn't get away from, this afternoon would be the right time after all.

Batten was holding on patiently.

"What do you want me to do?" Roger asked at last.

"Well, if we could get these photographs developed quickly — those of the couple with Caldicott, I mean — and send them up to you, it might help. They might be only interested buyers but last night they told me they were just passing through and wouldn't stay for the actual auction. That could be Lie Number One. Could I send the photos up for you to look at?"

"Yes," Roger decided. "And I'll have one of our specialists in art thefts to have a look at them. How will your chap come."

"As a matter of fact, sir, it's a young woman, Detective Officer Linda Prell," Batten told him. "She'll come up by road on her own, Mr. West — she's off duty this afternoon so she can be semi-official, too. Shall I send her straight to you at the Yard? She should arrive by half-past three."

"Yes, do that," Roger said, and soon rang off on Batten's over-enthusiastic expressions of appreciation.

He dialled Kempton but someone else answered, left a message for the Chief Inspector to call him, and then pondered Batten's insistence as well as the reputation of the man Caldicott. Batten would not have pushed so hard unless he felt pretty certain there was good cause, but for some reason he didn't want to consult his superiors yet.

Roger smiled; but then, in his present mood it did not need much to make him smile.

*   *   *

Earlier that day Sarah and Neil Stephenson stood at the back of Leech's Gallery as Caldicott walked round, examining a great number of pictures with extraordinary care. The pictures were crowded together, some of the frames touching, because there was so little room. Dealers from London as well as Bristol, Birmingham, Bournemouth and Southampton were there with a great number of runners from all over England. The pictures were on show prior to auction, at a nearby hotel — the Hart, not the Rose and Briar. Special parking arrangements had been made by the police so that the grounds of the big new College of Further Education were being used as well as the car park of the Hart Hotel. If one turned, one could see a distant view of the cathedral spire beneath a sun already high. There were no clouds anywhere.

Hovering among the crowd of twenty or thirty people was a dark-haired girl in her early twenties.

She wore a flowered linen two-piece suit and linen hat, carried a linen handbag and wore shoes covered with the same linen; somehow all of these things tended to make her look as if she was on holiday. Now and again she was very close to Caldicott; and now and again very close to the Stephensons. Her collar was high at the neck, covering the chain of a heavy locket, the kind in which Victorians kept photographs of great sentimental value. She fiddled with this frequently, as if the catch was loose and she was afraid of losing it.

Stephenson gripped Sarah's arm just after this young woman had passed them. She was now standing by Caldicott, and fiddling yet again with the locket. Stephenson bent close to Sarah, and whispered:

"The girl in the linen suit is taking photographs of us and of Frankie. Did you know?"

Sarah asked in a languid voice which carried to several people nearby:

"Are you sure?"

"You know I'm sure."

"Then what are you going to do about it?" asked Sarah, more softly.

Stephenson didn't answer, but turned towards the door, which was propped open because the room was so hot and stuffy. A bluebottle flew in and buzzed on a vicious note; flies hovered in the doorway on their senseless, pattern-less flight. Stephenson walked past the window and Sarah pretended to take no notice; instead, she looked about the paintings and the people, then focused her gaze on Caldicott until he turned to look at her. The girl in the flowered linen was on one side, apparently oblivious, yet she kept glancing at the door.

Stephenson came back, after ten minutes. By that time Caldicott was by Sarah, and his expression betrayed the fact that Sarah had told him what Stephenson suspected.

"You two stay in here," Stephenson said. "I've some things to fix. Don't come out until I return for you."

If Caldicott resented the way this was said, he showed no sign; but there was a glow in his eyes as Stephenson went out; and he took Sarah's arm.

"There's a lovely Turner over in the corner," he declared. "Come and see."

There was more life to Sarah's face in the next few minutes than often showed for hours on end. Neither of them noticed the girl in flowered linen go out.

Stephenson was gone for twenty minutes, during which time a little group of Japanese came in, and, soon afterwards, John Withers. Withers had obviously seen the collection before and was simply putting in an appearance. Leech, who seemed to be in a dozen places at once, spent only a minute with him, then approached the Japanese.

"Good morning," one of these said. "We are from the Kyoto Gallery in Japan. We were in London and we heard . . ."

His voice faded as Withers came up to Sarah and Caldicott, was very amiable, hoped they would find time to visit him, and was then called aside by a friend.

More and more people arrived, and finally Stephenson returned and said at once:

"Let's go."

Caldicott's lips tightened; he was obviously annoyed by the other's peremptory manner.

"What's all this about being photographed?" he asked brusquely. "Are you sure?"

"Sure enough not to take chances," answered Stephenson. He was breathing hard, as if very agitated. "You go straight back to London, Frankie. I'll call you at your flat, and pay you later."

"Neil —" began Caldicott stiffly.

"That's it. That's everything," Stephenson said sharply.

"Don't you even want a report on those pictures? They're absolutely genuine."

"Forget them," ordered Stephenson. "This is a job we don't do. If I had a market for a million dollars I wouldn't touch these paintings now. You catch your train and don't worry about a thing.

"Do what he says, Frank, please," urged Sarah.

Caldicott looked from one to the other, saw they were adamant, shrugged, and walked on. He felt strangely solitary, and he knew it was chiefly because of Sarah. He had wanted to spend the rest of the day with her, even sharing her with Stephenson; he felt as enchanted as he had been yesterday. He knew better than to look round but in the window of a shop he saw their reflection. He wondered what had disturbed Stephenson so much; whether the girl with the locket camera had been enough to change his mind about his plans, or whether he had ever been really serious about the pictures here.

Could that have been a blind, to hide some other purpose?

Caldicott did not dwell on that thought, but neither did he dismiss it. The whole affair had disgruntled him, and by far the worst part of it was that he was unlikely ever to see Sarah again.

5

Capture

DETECTIVE OFFICER LINDA PRELL was a dedicated police-woman who had served in the uniformed branch, doing every kind of sordid job, for three years. She was young in years but old in experience except experience in actual detective work. When she had discussed this job with Tom Batten early this morning, she had suggested the locket camera, which she had used once before. It had not occurred to her that any of her subjects would realise what she was doing.

Now, following Stephenson at a discreet distance, she saw him go into the main doors of the Hart Hotel where the auction was to be held next day. This hotel, the largest in Salisbury, was two miles or more from the Rose and Briar, and had its parking and garage space spread over a wide area.

Linda Prell slipped into the car park.

She knew the hotel's many annexes and entrances. There were some rooms on the ground floor here, and a man whom she had seen talking to Stephenson that morning had one of these. She went in by a side entrance then saw the man through the window of his room.

He was at the telephone, and she could just hear him through the open window.

She went closer but kept out of sight; and she heard him say:

"Yes, you can use this room, Mr. Stephenson. Sure, that's all right. A pleasure."

The telephone tinged as he replaced it. He moved out of

the room and she heard the door close. She stepped away from the window and hurried towards an entrance used mostly by residents coming for their cars. The man did not appear. She hesitated, then acted on the spur of the moment, going closer to the window again and standing so that she couldn't be seen.

Soon, Stephenson came in with another man whom she couldn't see. They began to talk like old friends; the second man's voice was English, and familiar but she couldn't place it. She listened intently, relying on her memory and not making notes.

"It's too big a deal to take any chances with," the Englishman was saying. "If anything goes wrong I'm in very deep already."

"No one is stopping you from selling some paintings," said the American. "A lot of those you've got are cool enough by now, you'll miss the market if you don't sell before long."

"I'll miss the market if I let you sell too soon," the Englishman remarked drily.

Stephenson laughed.

"Okay, so no one makes a monkey out of you. But this big deal could make or break even Nicodemus!"

Both men laughed, the Englishman on a wry note before he replied: "You've got Ledbetter at the ready and this electronics man on your hook, you say."

"I certainly have."

"I've got my end sewn up, I can have the loot out of the country within an hour of it being stolen," said the Englishman.

Linda *knew* she would recognise the voice eventually but recollection still evaded her. Not that it mattered! Stephenson was the key, once she was able to report.

Suddenly, before she could do anything to get away, a car swung into the car park, hemming her against the wall. The driver was the man from the bedroom, in chauffeur's uniform. Linda moved to one side but the chauffeur moved to block her. At the same moment the door of the car was opened, and he ordered:

"Get in."

"I certainly won't get in!"

He drew a knife from his pocket, the blade very bright, and repeated: "Get in if you don't want your throat cut."

For the first time in her life, she was afraid.

There was not only the knife, but the expression in his eyes which convinced her that he would use it. She knew every kind of move in self-defence, but for the open door and the position in which he stood she would have taken a chance at attacking him. As it was, she stood very still, not quite sure what to do.

A man appeared from inside the back of the car, and gripped her wrist.

"Get *in*," the chauffeur ordered.

He moved the knife. The man in the car pulled. She found herself dragged into the car, now utterly unable to help herself. The man in the car kept a grip on her wrist in such a way that she could not move but sat in an upright position. The chauffeur got into the front seat and started off. Leaving the car park, she saw him glance along the pavement and into the driving mirror, and then act with great unconcern. She half-turned her head but the man alongside her twisted her wrist enough to make her gasp.

"Oh!"

"Hurt you?"

"You — you know it hurt!"

"Hurt nothing," he sneered, "compared with what I could do." He twisted again and pain seared through her arm. "See what I mean?"

"What — what do you want?"

"Lucy Locket," the man answered.

She stared. "Lucy Locket —"

"That's right," he said. "Take off your locket, Lucy, and give it to me."

Her free hand flew to the locket and its metal chain, and she clutched and covered it, until the man hoisted her left hand again and the pain become unbearable. She screamed out but they were going fast along a country road and no one was in sight or earshot. Her fear was greater because of a sense of helplessness and because she was over the first shock and knew that this was really happening.

"Gimme the locket," the man ordered.

She fumbled with the clasp at the back of her neck, and now began to think more rationally. Her fear had not subsided but was under control. The clasp came undone. If she could sling the heavy locket into the man's face, it might hurt enough to make him let her go. If it caught his eyes it could blind him, but whatever the risk she had to try.

He twisted viciously. She cried out, and the locket fell into her lap. She tried to strike him, but he fended the blow off and struck her savagely on the back of the neck with a chop of a blow. She gasped and doubled up, unconscious, as the man slid the locket from her lap. She crumpled up but he made no attempt at all to help her, just examined the locket. When it sprang open he saw the miniature camera inside and knew how right Stephenson had been. He leaned forward, holding the locket-camera out so that the chauffeur could see.

The man said: "That's bad."

"What shall I do?"

"Tell Neil."

"I mean with the girl."

"Ask Neil," the driver said, laconically.

"He doesn't pay us to ask him dumb questions," the man by Linda Prell said. "What are we going to do with her?"

"We could cut her throat," the driver remarked. "We weren't seen." He took his gaze off the road for a moment and glanced at the back of the unconscious woman's head. "Is she a cop?"

"I don't know."

"You can find out. If she's a cop she'll have her card."

The man who had taken the locket-camera put this into his pocket, and then opened the linen handbag. It had some money, photographs, a handkerchief and toilet accessories, but nothing at all to show her identity. He twisted her round so that he could pull at the neck of her dress, which opened with a zip fastener at the side. His hand felt the warm softness of her breasts, and a chain attached to a small packet in their valley. He drew the packet out, very slowly. It was a small purse, and inside was her warrant card and a tiny roll of film, not much larger than a pencil stub. He zipped up the dress again, and thrust the warrant card under the driver's nose.

"So she's a cop," the driver said, and this time he caught his breath. "That's bad."

"Si," the man behind him said, "what are we going to do with the bitch? And this time, don't tell me to talk to Neil. We've got a real live cop in the car, and she's seen us both. For all we know she's taken photographs of us both. What are we going to *do*?"

* * *

Detective Officer Linda Prell, just coming round, heard this, and heard everything that followed.

* * *

Simon Ledbetter, the driver of Stephenson's car, pulled off the road into a copse, reached by a narrow, leafy lane. No car was ahead and none in sight behind. Overhead, the sky was a clear, cloudless blue, and when he slowed down along the beech trees the sky seemed darker through the near-translucent leaves, not yet at full growth. When the car came to a standstill it was safely hidden from the highway. Only the insects buzzed and flew; and the birds.

"First," he said, "we make her talk."

"Doesn't the camera tell us all we want to know?"

"Sam," Ledbetter said. "We have to make her talk."

His voice made Linda Prell shiver. There had been something menacing in this particular man from the moment he had stopped her outside the Hart, and now the menace was much greater. She could not see him because she was crouched between the seats but she could remember him: small, compact, pale, hard-faced. His chauffeur's cap had been pulled at an angle over his left eye but she had seen the scar which ran from his eye towards his ear. The other man was younger, sharp-featured, ruddy-faced with fair hair. He had hurt her but he did not frighten her as did the other man.

She could not really believe she was here, in acute danger.

Only half-an-hour ago she had been in the hot and crowded gallery, feeling on top of the world, so sure that she was taking her photographs unnoticed. Now she was within an ace of death. That was not imagination; it was not melodramatic: it was literally true. The waves of panic swept over her like the waves of electric current but there was a part of her mind which was not taken over by fear; she could think. Reason told her that in the circumstances these men would have to kill her. She would be able to identify them, they hadn't a chance to escape if she were to live. So, she had no possible choice. She was going to die.

They were going to kill her.

But the driver, the hateful one of the pair, wanted to make her talk first.

She did not need telling the things he could do to cause pain; she had no doubt at all that if he tortured her she would not be able to hold out. So, she had to save herself from pain. That was the only thing she could do: save herself from pain.

It was no use trying to escape.

As that thought came, she asked despairingly: Isn't it?

If she ran, *could* she escape? She knew the countryside — goodness, she actually knew this copse! On the other side of the beeches there was a sandy ridge, pocked with rabbit holes and here and there a fox hole. The ground there fell away thirty or forty feet, the result of a landslide years ago, after torrential rain. In the landslide the roots of many of the trees had been bared, and today children often played among those gnarled and twisted roots. She could climb down and run across a field where barley already stood in massed spear formation, the shoots ankle high. Beyond the sloping field, beyond one of those smooth, green mounds which made Salisbury Plain so beautiful, was Webb's Farm, a thatched farmhouse and some nearby cottages. They couldn't be a mile away.

If she could only get there . . .

All these thoughts flashed through her mind while the men got out of the car and stood by it. They were in the middle of the copse, on the far side from the sandy ledge. She could creep out on the side away from them.

They were whispering.

She began to edge herself towards the door. It was closed and she would have to open it; how on earth could she open a car door without making enough noise to betray herself? She raised her head to look at the two men who were still whispering. Neither of them looked towards the car; they must think she was still unconscious. She turned the handle lever very slowly; it made no noise. She pushed the door open a crack and the sound was drowned by the cawing of a flock of rooks. She pushed it a further inch, almost hysterically grateful for the birds.

Then, she heard the driver say: "We must find out why she was sent."

"She doesn't have to have any special reason which affects us," the other argued. "How do you know they didn't send her to take pictures of everyone in the gallery?"

"What the hell do you mean?"

"Well, how do you know?" demanded the man from the back of the car. "She could have been sent to check on everyone."

"*He* doesn't think so."

"He could be wrong," the younger man screeched.

They were still for a moment, and Linda took in short, shallow breaths, but the rooks had circled away and no longer drowned any sound. The door was open wide enough for her to squeeze out, if only they didn't come round too soon. She pushed it a few inches wider but was suddenly faced with a problem: how to get out. She was on her knees, facing the door, and there was no room to turn round unless she first stood up: and they would see her. So her only hope was to crawl: to put her head and shoulders through, and her arms, and place both hands on the ground. She could do it. There would be no difficulty; all she needed was a little time.

Then the driver said: "So we'll ask her."

Oh God, no.

"And so we'll find out," he went on.

Footsteps crunched on beech mast, on last year's tough brown leaves. Twigs cracked. Birds flew, alarmed by the movement of men who had been standing so still. In panic,

Linda Prell tried to get out more quickly, she had one hand on the ground and the other touching when her skirt caught on the door handle, and she could not move. She could not move a hand to tug, could not even get leverage with her body. She made an effort, something ripped — and then, only a few feet from her, she saw a pair of feet; then another pair. One man gasped, the other man cried:

"You bitch!"

Then they moved stiffly and together. The younger man grabbed her by the shoulders and the other thrust into the car so that he could clutch her waist. She felt her dress tear, but she no longer thought of her clothes, or escape, or even life or death, she was simply afraid of pain.

"I'll tell you," she gasped. "I'll tell you!"

Somehow, they had placed her on her feet, against the trunk of a tree. The sun made a tracery of light and shadow on her face, even on her eyes. They acted as if they had rehearsed what they were doing. The young man went behind the tree and stretched round for her wrists, pulling her back against the tree so that she couldn't move.

And the driver stood in front of her.

She was gasping for breath. Her bosom was thrust forward. Her shoulder blades were grating on the bark of the tree. The driver took out the knife she had seen before, and she reached a screaming pitch of terror.

He said: "If you lie to me you'll wish you'd never been born." He paused for a moment and she could see every feature of his face including the scar, for he was not wearing his cap. It was a long, knotted scar, one which had been allowed to heal without being stitched. "Who sent you to take photographs?"

"My — my boss."

"*Who*, I said."

"Sergeant — Detective Sergeant Batten." When he didn't speak but waited as if for more information, she cried: "Tom Batten. It was Tom Batten."

"Whose picture were you to take?"

"There — there were three people, two men and a woman. Stephensons. And — the man's name was Caldicott. Caldicott."

"Who else?" demanded the driver. "Come on, let's have it. Who else?"

"No one," she gasped. "No one else, just those three!"

"Had you handed any film in?" he demanded.

"No. I hadn't even reloaded, I hadn't used up the first film."

"Who were you taking pictures of?"

"I've told you!" she cried. "A man named Stephenson and his wife, and a man named Caldicott. I've told you!"

"Why were you taking the pictures?" asked the driver, in a strong voice.

"I don't know! Tom Batten told me to, he's my superior officer. He —"

As she spoke, as she gasped for breath, she had a moment of tremendous relief, for the younger man released her arms and the awful strain was eased. She actually staggered forward, forgetting everything but the relief; forgetting even the driver's knife. Then she saw a glint at his hand, but it wasn't the knife, it was a hypodermic syringe.

"No!" she cried. "No, don't!"

She hardly felt pain as the needle slid into her arm.

6

Missing

TOM BATTEN LOOKED at his watch for the fifth or sixth time in ten minutes, and then went to the window of his small office in the new building at the Salisbury Police Station. A car was pulling in but it wasn't Linda's; and Linda should have been here at least an hour ago. It was nearly three o'clock, and the three people she had to photograph had been gone for over two hours. One, by train; the other two in a Jaguar which the man drove. These, the Stephensons, were heading for the West Country and Caldicott for London; he had caught the 12.31 according to the ticket-collector at the station.

Linda had left the shop just before eleven o'clock.

Why wasn't she here? Why hadn't she been back hours ago?

The assistant to Jacob Leech, a Miss Kuttle, had seen her leave but not known where she had gone. Two uniformed policemen and men in two patrol cars, told to pass the shop at regular intervals, had not seen her. Beyond this, Batten had made no inquiries but he knew that he would soon have to report to the Inspector-in-Charge. He had never been more troubled.

Another police car turned into the carriageway of the station, but still it wasn't Linda; he glanced at his watch again and saw that it was exactly three o'clock. He must report her as missing, at once. As he reached the Chief Inspector's office the door opened and Chief Inspector Isherwood himself came out. They bumped into each other.

"Sorry," grunted Isherwood.

"Sorry, sir," gasped Batten. "Can you —"

"Whatever it is must wait until later this afternoon, I'm late already." Isherwood, tall, dark, with a strong Lancashire accent, actually began to push past Batten, who dodged to let him pass and saw his large and at that moment uncompromising back. In a moment Isherwood would have started down the stairs.

"Sir!" cried Batten. "She's missing!"

Isherwood, if he heard, took no notice but turned the corner which led to the head of the stairs. Batten, feeling very cold, did not know what to do. One couldn't defy the Station Chief, and Isherwood —

Isherwood reappeared, asking as he turned the corner: "Who's missing?"

"Linda — Woman Police Constable Prell, sir."

"From that job at the Leech Gallery, you mean?"

"Yes, sir."

"Hasn't she been back?"

"No, sir."

"Nor telephoned?"

"No."

"Any idea what's happened to her?"

"No, sir," Batten said, and told the other exactly what he had done so far.

Isherwood stood unmoving. A head taller than the sergeant, he stared at the other with the kind of intensity which could throw a scare into a lesser man, but Batten matched his gaze. Another man came slowly and heavily up the stairs and turned the corner, almost bumped into Isherwood, backed and blurted: "Sorry, sir." It was one of the younger uniformed men at the station. Isherwood nodded and the man went along the passage to the offices, much more briskly.

"All right," Isherwood said. "It's absolute priority to find her. Have you put a general call out to all of our people?"

"No, sir."

"Do it. Then come back and see me." As Batten hurried past him and towards the stairs, the Chief Inspector opened a door and called out clearly: "Telephone the Mayor's secretary and give my apologies — urgent business has cropped up." The door banged, and Batttn did not hear anything else. Relieved by the seriousness with which Isherwood had reacted to the news, troubled by Linda's disappearance, deeply worried because he had taken so much into his own hands, Batten hurried to the Information Room, where three men sat at a desk with earphones clipped over their heads and another stood looking at a map.

"Please give exact location of the incident," one of the men was saying.

"Joe," Batten said to the man by the map, and the man turned as if in protest, saw Batten's expression and looked startled. "Joe," Batten said again, "I sent Linda out on a special job at Leech's this morning. She hasn't come back. The Old Man wants a general call put out for her."

Joe said: "What do you think's happened to her?"

"I wish I could guess. Will you make that Hampshire, Southampton, Bournemouth —"

"The lot," Joe promised, and he moved to a microphone standing on a long, narrow table, switched on, and said: "Salisbury 34 speaking, stand by for a general call." He motioned to Batten, covering the microphone as he whispered: "You do it. You know all about it."

Batten gulped; but when he began to speak his voice was as clear as it could be and the information he broadcast was both lucid and concise. The burden of it was simple: Woman Police Constable Linda Prell, last seen at Leech's Gallery, Salisbury, wearing a flowered linen suit and...was wanted for urgent consultations at Salisbury Police Headquarters. All officers were to assist in finding her and giving her this message.

*   *   *

From mouth to mouth, telephone to telephone, radio to radio, the message was passed, and with it a mood of concern. Echoed and re-echoed throughout the county and neighbouring police districts were words and phrases of alarm.

"That's a queer one," a man would say.

"That means she's missing."

"Why wouldn't she report if she could?"

"There's trouble here, don't you make any mistake."

And everywhere the police began their probe, in Salisbury and far beyond. But there was no report, not even of a metallic-blue Capri into which Linda Prell had disappeared. Her car was in the car park of the Hart Hotel, where she had taken it before going to the preview. There was simply disquiet, increasing as every half-hour passed without any news.

*   *   *

Roger West was back at his desk, working more intensively, by three o'clock. The elation of the morning remained, but two things had occurred to him. If this new job was to be officially created soon his desk must be as clear as he could get it; and if he was to handle the job well, he must be given some clear terms of reference. Largely because he could not discuss it with anybody, he was beginning to feel tension building up out of impatience to know more. There had never been a time when he needed a job to get his teeth into. There was just a possibility that the visit from the woman police officer from Salisbury would give him a stimulus. By half-past three, he began to wait for news that she had arrived. At twenty to four, the inter-office telephone rang, and he lifted the receiver almost as a reflex action.

"West."

"The Commander," Coppell said; he had a voice which vibrated uncomfortably over the microphone.

News of the new job? "Yes, sir?"

"Have you had a young woman officer to see you from Wiltshire?"

"One's due to see me at any time," Roger answered, taken completely by surprise. "How did you know?"

"It's a garbled story," said Coppell, "and I can't wait to help sort it out. But Sir Richard Way, the Chief Constable for the South-West Federation, has asked for help. Apparently this girl hasn't reported for some hours. May be a false alarm, may be something to worry about. Wiltshire think it is. Go down there right away, will you?"

"I'll be off in —" Roger began, and then exclaimed: "One other thing, sir."

"What?"

"Chief Inspector Kempton knows as much as anybody about Caldicott. I'd like to —"

"If you want him, take him," Coppell interrupted. "Take anything and anyone you need." He put the receiver down heavily, obviously very much in a hurry.

Roger dialled Kempton's number on the inter-office machine. It rang for some seconds before a man answered:

"Chief Inspectors' office."

"Mr. Kempton, please."

"Half a mo'," the man said, and then called in an echoing voice: "Alan! Telephone."

Roger held on. The call, the situation in the office where five Chief Inspectors worked together reminded him vividly of his own early days as a comparatively senior officer. There had been a camaraderie which echoed over the telephone now as well as down the years. Once a superintendency and one's own office was achieved a barrier came up which was never really broken down. Roger's closest friends among superintendents were men he had known in his C.I. days. What put one on one's own? Responsibility?

Another voice sounded.

"Sorry to keep you, I had —"

"This is Superintendent West," Roger interrupted. "How long will it take you to be ready to drive to Salisbury with me?"

There was only a moment's hesitation; a hush, as if that barrier was descending, before Kempton answered:

"Five minutes, sir."

That was just the response Roger would have made to the same question twenty — it was *twenty!* — years ago.

"We'll use my car," Roger decided. "It will be outside the Victoria Street entrance." He rang off on whatever remark Kempton made, then dialled the garage to have his car sent round. Next, he put his head round the communicating door, and caught Venables, the tall sergeant, breaking a piece of chocolate at his mouth. "I'm going to Salisbury," he said, "and taking Chief Inspector Kempton with me."

"*Verumph goo', sir.*" Part of the chocolate disappeared in a gulp. "Sorry, sir!"

Roger waved his hand in a 'forget it' gesture, and went out. Dodging back into his office he picked up his bag, rather like a doctor's bag and containing everything he was likely to want in an investigation; experience had taught him not to rely on getting what he needed at other police stations. This bag was always ready and he did not need to check it. He crossed to the door and his inter-office telephone rang. "Damn!" he exclaimed, but a moment's delay wasn't really important, and he crossed to it. "West!"

"Sorry to worry you, sir," said Kempton. "Shall I bring my bag?"

"Yes," Roger said. "One should, always."

"Right, sir!"

Five minutes later, Roger was by the side of his car, a dark blue Rover-3-litre, when Kempton came striding from the corner of Broadway, having come the long way round. He carried a rather larger bag than Roger's, black and metal-edged. He was a man of medium height but Roger had forgotten how very broad and thickset he was; and had forgotten how tough-looking, with heavy features and a broken nose. Something, probably the dark blue eyes deep beneath the jutting black eyebrows, softened his face. His jaw was massive, with a deep cleft.

"Sorry to keep you, sir."

"If I never had to wait for anyone longer than that, I wouldn't have anything to complain about," Roger responded. "Go round the other side." He took the wheel, and soon he was weaving through the traffic towards Victoria and the south and south-west. "I can't tell you very much because there isn't much to tell. Salisbury sent a request for help, and they wouldn't have done that if they weren't badly worried." He explained all he knew, and then asked: "What would you do next?"

"Pick up Caldicott?" suggested Kempton.

"I think we should trace him and watch him," Roger

said. "It's too early to pick him up. Odd," he added to himself. "Usually we're called in too late, this time we've been called before a crime has been committed, as far as I can see." When Kempton didn't speak, he went on: "Do you know Salisbury?"

"Slightly," answered Kempton. "I was down there two years ago when they had the robbery from the local castle. We were lucky — picked up the man and found a Rubens and Tintoretto he'd taken. The Inspector-in-Charge was a Manchester man, Jack Isherwood."

"It still is," Roger said.

"Good!"

"Is he all right?"

"First-class man to work with, sir, yes."

"I'm glad to hear it. Do you know a Detective Sergeant Batten?"

Kempton gave an explosive chuckle, then glanced quickly at Roger to check whether the laugh was acceptable. Was he, Roger West, supposed to be such a humourless creature? Kempton looked straight ahead, and said:

"Man rather like a porker to look at?"

"I know what you mean," Roger said. "How good is he?"

"I'd say very good indeed, sir, but a bit of a lone wolf. Often being called over the coals for doing things off his own bat." Now Kempton's look at Roger was almost sly. "I don't just mean that in emergency he would make snap decisions, but he has a tendency to follow his own line of reasoning and to plan an investigation, as it were, without consulting anyone else. Quite a character, sir."

Alan Kempton seemed to be a good judge of men.

"It looks as if he's been at it again," Roger said. "We'll soon see. Arrange for Caldicott to be watched, will you?"

Immediately, Kempton took the radio-telephone off its hook and gave instructions to the Yard. Then he sat back, and Roger concentrated on his driving. Twice during the next two hours word came through that there was no news of Linda Prell. Roger saw Kempton looking about him at the rolling countryside, obviously enjoying the drive, while he himself took much of it in as he drove. There were few parts of the country he liked better.

They were leaving Stockbridge by the steep hill, just going off the dual carriageway, when a Ford Capri, a metallic-blue colour which showed very bright in the sun, swept past a Morris Minor and went on to the new section of the motorway towards London.

In the boot of that car was Linda Prell.

*   *   *

"Not a word, not a sign," Isherwood said when they were in his office, just after half-past five. "Everyone has been alerted. We haven't broadcast that she's missing yet but we've asked local farmworkers and farmers to keep a lookout for anything unusual. So far, nothing at all's turned up. Linda Prell walked out of Leech's and vanished. It's as simple as that, crazy as it sounds." He looked from Roger to Kempton, and went on: "I think it's time we questioned Caldicott and the Stephensons. I hope you agree, Mr. West."

Roger asked: "Do you know where the Stephensons are?"

"Yes. In Bath, at the Pump Hotel," Isherwood answered. "We could send someone there or we could bring them back here," he went on. "Which do you think is better?"

Roger gave Kempton a moment or two in which to speak, and then answered: "I'd like to know who else was in the gallery this morning: who else might have thought the police-woman was taking pictures of them. I don't think we should take it for granted that the Stephensons and Caldicott are involved. Will you be satisfied if we have them watched?" He turned on all his charm as he smiled at Isherwood.

"No," answered the Salisbury man promptly. "But I'll settle for it! And Jacob Leech, who owns the gallery, can probably tell you who else was there. Have you done anything about the man Caldicott?"

"He's being watched," Kempton answered very quickly. "If we need him we can pick him up any time we like, sir."

"I wish to God we could say the same of Linda Prell," growled Isherwood.

7

Cool Nerve

NEIL STEPHENSON SAT in a lounge at the Pump Hotel, in
Bath, watching the television news. Sarah sat by his side,
dressed in an ice-blue suit which made her seem even more
aloof, apart, from everyone else. Most people who came into
the lounge glanced at her but she encouraged no one to look
twice. The B.B.C. announcer was his usual bland self, the
reporters covered various items of news including a fête at
Bristol with their customary assurance. Then suddenly a
photograph was thrown on to the screen, and both Neil
Stephenson and Sarah sat up and stared intently.

"One of the biggest manhunts ever staged in the south-west
of England began in Salisbury, Wiltshire, late this afternoon," the announcer said. "Here is John Wilberforce with
on-the-spot details." His voice faded, another man's replaced
it, brisker, and with a hint of Wiltshire accent.

"The photograph on your screens," he said promptly, "is
that of Linda Prell of the Salisbury Division of the Wiltshire
Constabulary. Woman Police Constable Prell vanished this
morning after being at an art gallery — the Leech Gallery
where I am now standing — where some Old Masters were
on preview, prior to auction . . ."

The picture changed.

The reporter stood in front of the shop with his microphone round his neck, showing some of the paintings in the
window. There were close-ups of the Constables and a
Turner, an interview with bearded Leech, mostly explanation
of the way the pictures had been discovered: ". . . the

treasures have been hidden in this isolated Wiltshire farm-house for at least a hundred years ..." There was another change of picture and a sweeping view of the cathedral spire over the old tiled roofs of nearby buildings. "Now the quiet of this lovely cathedral city has been shattered by the disappearance of the young woman police officer. The Wiltshire Police regard her disappearance as of such impor-tance that they have asked Scotland Yard for help ... Chief Superintendent Roger West arrived late this afternoon ..."

Roger's picture appeared on the screen, and the reporter asked:

"Have you been able to discover any clue to explain the missing officer's disappearance, Superintendent?"

"No," Roger answered.

Behind him hovered Isherwood and Batten, a discreet distance from the microphone and the camera.

"Has any motive yet been discovered?"

"None is yet proved," Roger West answered briskly. "But there has been very little time. The Salisbury Police haven't lost a minute."

"Is there anything the public can do to help in the search?" demanded the reporter.

"Yes indeed," West said, and his face was brought into close-up so that he appeared to be almost in the room where the Stephensons sat. Everyone was watching intently except an elderly man whose newspaper kept rustling over a stomach which rose and fell rhythmically. "Every man and woman in Salisbury, in Wiltshire, in the neighbouring counties can search their memories for this young woman ..."

His picture faded; a very large blow-up of Linda Prell's replaced it.

"We need to trace this policewoman's movements from the time she was seen to leave Leech's Gallery at about ten forty-five this morning," Roger West went on. "A local newspaperman saw her go. Meanwhile every available police officer and several military units will begin a search at dawn tomorrow ... The help of the public is urgently required ... Farmers and farmworkers are particularly requested to report anything even slightly unusual. A car parked in an unusual place, for instance: reports of noises: cigarette ends, pieces of litter, anything which might have been left in a copse, a corner of a field, in a shed or empty house . . ."

At last, the appeal was over.

Soon, the newscast ended in a brief forecast about the next day's weather. Stephenson touched Sarah's knee and they went out of the room in silence, then up to their rooms: communicating rooms with a bathroom in between. Stephenson put an evening newspaper on the foot of a double bed.

Sarah said: "Do you know anything about that woman police officer?"

"Sarah, how could you say such a thing!"

"Neil," she said, "I'm not a fool. I saw you go out, and I know that Ledbetter, the man who drives you in London, was staying in the next room. If he killed her —"

"Don't be ridiculous, honey," Stephenson interrupted. "And don't interfere with things that don't concern you."

"What happens if the police come after us?" demanded Sarah, speaking with more feeling than she had yet shown.

"We tell them we don't know a thing, which we don't. And if I knew anything I wouldn't tell you, so you needn't lie, hon. Ledbetter works for a car rental company which rents me a car whenever I'm in London, and a self-drive for the country. So what is there to say we're involved?"

"*You* are involved," she corrected icily.

"If I am, you, Frankie and all of us are," said Stephenson harshly. "We don't know a thing and we don't say a thing. We stay here until tomorrow and we look at some picture galleries and some antique shops. We just act normal, and don't you make any mistake." He looked at her levelly, coldly: "You understand that, Sarah?"

She said: "I suppose you know that there isn't a chance of getting any of those paintings in Salisbury. That's what you came for, isn't it?"

He said: "Is it?" and the question hovered in the air. There was a strange expression on his face, one she had seldom seen. He went on as if he had not posed the question, saying: "We didn't have a chance once the police began to take those photographs. From that moment we had to lay off the paintings job."

"So coming this way was a waste of time," Sarah said.

5—TTOMC * *

"Waste of time?" echoed Stephenson. "Is that what you think?" He gave a sudden grin, showing his small teeth, and rubbed her cheek with his forefinger. "It's a good thing I didn't bring you along for your brains, honey!"

She asked flatly: "What is that supposed to mean? What are you really up to? Don't try to put me off by saying if I don't know anything I can't talk. I want to know what you mean."

"It means you don't know a good thing when you see one."

"*What* good thing?"

"Honey," he said, cupping her chin between his thumb and forefinger, "you want to know, so okay, you can know. We didn't come down here for those paintings, we came for something real big." His grip became so tight it hurt but she did not move or protest. "We talked about it last night. That Magna Carta. Boy, that's the McCoy!" He released her and moved to the foot of the bed and sat down. "Yes, ma'am, that's so big I dream about it."

"You couldn't be such a fool as to touch that!" Anger sparked in her eyes, and she took a step forward.

"Not right now, honey, not right now," breathed Stephenson. "But the time will soon come. I checked on that Magna Carta this morning, while Frankie was showing you the town. And I called Nicodemus in New York."

"You called him from *here*?"

"That's right," said Stephenson, sounding almost gay. "He had asked me what chance there was to get the M.C. I had news for him. I told him there was talk of some of the other twelve turning up, but this was the McCoy, and it's the one Old Nick wants. You want to know what he said? He said I could name my own price. He said he could get three or four of the big collectors competing for it. He said —" Stephenson's eyes held a seraphic light, and he placed his hands on Sarah's shoulders and drew her close. "You can talk in millions, honey — millions of dollars. That's how much of a waste of time it was coming to this part of the world. That's how dumb I am!"

Sarah didn't move, didn't yield, just stared up at him, lips parted a little, showing a glimpse of teeth.

"You *are* crazy," she exclaimed.

"You agree with an expert, honey!"

"You could never get away with it."

"You'll see," Stephenson said. "You'll surely see."

"Neil." She almost choked on the name.

"Yes, honey?"

"Millions?"

"Yes, honey."

"It — it's impossible." Her voice faltered.

"Not to me," he assured her. "Nothing is impossible to me."

"How — how would you do it?"

"Now, sweetheart," Stephenson said in his most expansive mood, "you know better than to ask me a question like that."

"Neil," she said, "if we ever go back to Salisbury they'll watch us all the time."

"So?"

"So how could you possibly —"

"Honey," Stephenson said, "I'll find a way. I'm going back to li'l ole U.S.A. to talk with Nicodemus and maybe some of the others asd then I'm going to find me a man who can open the way to that library where they keep the Magna Carta. Don't make any mistake. There's one at Lincoln and two in the British Museum but the Salisbury one is the big apple. The Sarum Magna Carta, they call it. I've been reading about it. We can be over the Atlantic with it out of London Airport before they'll know it's missing. It can be out of that library and in some collector's strong room in twenty-four hours, or less, honey, or less." He paused for a few moments and then said: "Now, I want to think."

He released her, and she backed away.

"You could never do it," she said. "Not now or any time."

"I'll do it, hon, don't you worry. And it will be worth millions."

She looked at him and realised that she had never seen such a rapt expression on his face; this concept really fired him. She had known him for years but this was her first long trip with him. She was not sure but had come to believe he was a consummate liar; that it was never wise to believe a word he said. She was tempted to ask more questions but controlled herself, and moved towards the bath-room.

"Are you sure you don't want me to stay?"

"Not tonight, honey," Stephenson said, apologetically. "I tell you I want to think, and you distract me when I want to think. Goodnight, sweetheart."

She went into and across the bathroom and to her own, smaller room, furnished with shiny mahogany, tall mirrors, high ceilings, silk curtains. She turned the key in the lock of the door and went across to the further of the two beds. She curled up on this, and ate several chocolates from a box on the dressing-table as she thought more about Neil. The longer she thought, the more she felt that he was not only cunning but Machiavellian in his thinking. It was impossible to be sure what was going on in his mind.

He couldn't be sure what was going on in hers, either. She lifted the telephone and gave a London number. Soon, the operator called her back, and a man said:

"Who is that?"

"Frank," she said, "you know who it is."

"My God," he exclaimed. "Where are you?"

"In Bath."

"You shouldn't have called —"

"It's all right," she interrupted. "He's in his room and I shan't see him again tonight. He's having a thinking session!"

"He's got plenty to think about," Caldicott said drily.

"Frank," she said, "if you are asked any questions just say you came to advise him about the paintings."

"Well, that's what I did," Caldicott answered.

"You want to know something?"

"Yes," Caldicott said.

"That was a blind. He had us fooled, he really came down to check on another thing."

There was a pause, as if Caldicott was puzzled, but suddenly he drew in a gasping breath, and said:

"You mean he's after a bigger job and used the paintings to explain why he was in Salisbury? He must be mad!"

"The word most used is crazy," Sarah said drily. "Do you remember last night when we were all talking by the river?"

When Caldicott didn't answer at once she lowered her voice to a seductive level, and repeated: "Do you remember last night?"

Roughly, he answered: "I shall never forget it."

"And nothing happened," she said.

"Everything happened to me."

"Frank — think for a moment."

"I think about nothing else," Caldicott said. "You, and that lunatic!"

"Don't put anything into words," she warned, "but do you remember what we were talking about?"

"Last night?"

"Yes."

"Several things," he said.

"One of a dozen," she replied, gently.

"One of a dozen what? I — *oh!*" There was a sudden change in his tone, and an explosive: *"That?"*

"I see you don't forget things," Sarah said. "The piece of history. Do you remember?"

"I remember. What has that got to do with —" He broke off again.

"He's got an interested buyer," Sarah said. "Do you remember when I asked him whether he meant pounds or dollars?" Caldicott gave a choky laugh as she went on: "I gather it could be pounds."

Caldicott caught his breath.

"Do you see what I mean?" asked Sarah.

"We couldn't possibly get it."

"He thinks he can. So you be very careful."

"I tell you he's mad!"

"No," Sarah said, "not on this kind of thing. There is a great deal I could tell you about Neil's weaknesses, but being wrong or careless about a big project isn't one of them. He's convinced that it can be done, and that means there is a way. Don't be surprised at anything he asks you."

"Asks *me*."

"You're his chief contact in England," she pointed out. "He'll be in touch with you when this paintings affair has blown over. Don't put him off, Frank — not if you want to see me again."

After a long pause, Caldicott said: "We'll be damned lucky if we don't spend the next —" He broke off, choking, and it was a long time before she spoke.

"Frank," she said, "you'll be all right. Just keep your nerve. You came to value some pictures for Neil, to tell him whether you thought they were real or fakes. That's all. When you'd done your job you went back home. There's absolutely nothing to worry about," she went on. "And Neil has a really big idea. I want to share in the proceeds, and then he and I can part company. Just be patient."

"I know," Caldicott said. "I should be. But I can't bear to think of you sleeping with that —"

"Don't talk so," Sarah rebuked. "My body is mine, and I don't find it difficult to sleep with Neil or anyone who can give me a luxury trip like this. There's no love in it, don't you understand that? It doesn't mean a thing to me with him, but with you —" She broke off. "Have *you* been a celibate all your life? Even the past six months?"

She broke off, and there was no sound but his breathing. When he didn't reply she whispered: "Goodnight, Frank," and rang off.

*   *   *

Caldicott felt as if Sarah's breath actually touched his cheek, his ear, as she said: "Goodnight, Frank." He hardly heard the receiver go down and could not believe she had gone. "Sarah!" he called pleadingly, and repeated: "Sarah!" But she did not reply. He put the receiver down slowly, and sat very still, until suddenly he exclaimed: "It's impossible!" He paused again and then went on: "I mustn't let myself be obsessed by her." He was silent again, then switched his thoughts. "No one in their senses would plan to steal Magna Carta." He stood up and began to pace the large room with its oddments of furniture, some good, some worth practically nothing. He lived in this small flat alone and there was untidiness everywhere; hardly a surface without dust on which one could draw finger pictures.

He stood still, looking at an old print of London before the first great fire which had razed the city when the

Salisbury cathedral was already over three hundred years old; it was one of his treasures.

"Magna Carta," he breathed. "Impossible!"

Yet he stared at the old print, and then spun round and took a book off a wide shelf: *Rulers of England*. He flipped over the pages until he came to a full plate picture: the Lincoln Magna Carta. On one side was the original York copy; on the opposite plate a copy of the translation, on what appeared to be parchment.

"It's impossible," he breathed again.

It wasn't until later that he realised that for nearly an hour he had forgotten the police search for Linda Prell.

8

No Trace

ON HIS SECOND DAY in Salisbury Roger West stood at the window of the King's Arms, a small hotel overlooking the eastern wall of the cathedral. Oak beams supported wall and ceiling, beams which had been placed in position over four hundred years ago. Not far along this same road, a main highway to the west of England, was the Hart Hotel from which Linda Prell had disappeared. Two miles beyond the cathedral and the River Avon was the Rose and Briar, which he had not yet visited.

Towering above wall and buildings was the slender, graceful spire. He could almost hear Batten saying:

"And believe it or not, a hundred years after the cathedral was built, another bishop came along and had that spire put on top. The original tower was squat as any Norman church one, anyone would have said there wasn't a hope of the spire staying put. But it did. Wonderful builders and engineers they had in those days. Anyone who tried to do what old Dick Farleigh did back in the fourteenth century would be called a fool."

And there it rose into the sky.

There was magic in both the spire and the building, magic which lured him out of the hotel and along to Queen Anne's Gate, an entrance to the close only for pedestrians.

Beyond the old stone wall which surrounded the cathedral sweeping lawns were covered with huge patches of daisies and buttercups, already closing their petals, for the evening was chill. One great cedar tree lorded it over younger, smaller beech and chestnut and elm. But it was the building itself, so massive and yet so delicately wrought, in which the stone seemed to be part of a tight-knit lacery; there were the buttresses standing alone and yet part of a whole which had such grandeur. The arched windows, some of stained glass given brightness by sunlight which shone through windows on the far side, and the small spires — turrets might be a better word — seemed to point upwards not to the sky but to the tower and its spire. Beyond and to his right were many houses of weathered red brick and some of stone, and gates of wrought iron. One was clad in a mass of wisteria which the sun caught and seemed to trap as if it were stolen from the sky.

Roger walked from this north-eastern corner towards the northern porch and the western doors, where the carved figures of saints and patriarchs had survived Cromwell's onslaught, softened in this place by a commander who had reverenced beauty and tradition as much as he had been loyal to the soldier of change. He passed the entrance to the cloisters, from which two boys came running, eight or nine perhaps, reminding him vividly of his own sons as they had been fifteen years ago. In the cloisters he could see more green beyond the many delicate arches; a cedar of Lebanon and another tree he did not recognise stood on this lawn, branches intertwined like the fingers of lovers.

At last, reluctantly, he turned away from contemplation of the stone; and, soon, away from the old houses facing the west entrance. He made himself walk back quickly, nodding to the security officer and the close constable, still helping the tourists who flocked here, guiding car drivers, answering the searching questions of hippy-like youths. He heard the security officer say:

"I know they say there are four of them but there are only three and a half, really — one was damaged by fire. And I've heard that the one at Lincoln was damaged when they photographed it by infra red . . ."

His voice faded.

Tom Batten had told him, Roger, of that and of much more when they had walked round, earlier in the evening.

Love for the cathedral and for the Sarum Magna Carta echoed in this man's voice as it had in Batten's.

"There's a group of us who are worried about the safety of all the old manuscripts in the library," Batten had said. "Why there's a Gallican Psalter there, written in Latin but with Saxon words between the lines. Would you believe it!" And Batten would not be satisfied until he had taken Roger into the cathedral and across to the library entrance, up the stone spiral staircase to the library itself. At one end of a long display case a group of people were listening to a very old woman who was talking of the Sarum Magna Carta with as much reverence as if she were praying. Whispering, Batten pointed to the psalter, in a triangular glass case with a thermometer beside it.

"That's to check the temperature," he had said. "These old vellums mustn't get too hot or too cold. *Look*. There's the Saxon writing. Do you see? That was the language of the country then. Hardly anyone but Saxon scholars can read it, but *thousands* can read the Latin which practically no one spoke in those days."

"How is it you know so much?" Roger had asked him.

"Always fascinated me even when I was a choir boy here," Batten had answered. "And I've been one of the special security guards for years. A few of us take turns to keep an eye on the place at night. Why, I could show you . . ."

A message had come for Roger to call Scotland Yard and the library had closed a special late opening before he had been able to see the precious Magna Carta itself.

"It'll be back in the safe by the time we could get back," Batten had said. "I'll show it to you tomorrow."

When Roger had returned to the King's Arms it had been nearly seven o'clock. Now, it was almost ten.

Nothing sensational had happened at the auction; the Old Masters had not reached their reserve and would next go to London salerooms; but high prices had been obtained for the rest of the paintings and Leech, who impressed Roger as very shrewd, had sold at least a dozen pictures from his own stock.

The Stephensons and Caldicott had been remarkable only by their absence.

Kempton was still out with a search party sweeping across some of the hills and through copses, because two farm-workers had reported a car parked off the road the previous day; and repeated, also, that the wind had carried the sound of a woman's voice as she cried:

"No, don't, no!"

They had thought it was an unwilling woman who had taken too great a chance. When asked why they hadn't gone to investigate, one, a man of forty or so with a wind-reddened face and distance-calmed eyes had said simply:

"No business of mine, were it? In any case I couldn't have got there in time to stop un, even if he'd be stopped." And then the eyes had crinkled and the voice had cackled: "Take more than that to stop me if I was anywhere near, that I'll tell you."

Roger, drawn again to his room window, was thinking of that now.

It wasn't callousness; it was simply acceptance of the way of the world. If a girl went with a man she couldn't trust, then who was to blame for what happened? Another thought hovered at the back of his mind: that in this age of permissiveness, when comparatively few girls were virgins until their marriage, the old customs died hard. One was still shocked by rape; all his life as a policeman hadn't hardened him to that. And once a girl found the man she wanted, she used all the old tricks to get him to the altar. Whatever the intellectuals and the pseudo-intellectuals said, marriage was still the ultimate aim of most young women. And men, for that matter. It was still the way of society and if it changed would change slowly and almost imperceptibly.

He turned back from the window.

That kind of semi-philosophical pondering would get him nowhere. He had this job on his plate, and the fact that he was away from London didn't alter the fact that he was obviously in charge. All eyes, then, were on him.

Did all eyes see what he sensed? That he had slipped up?

A whole day had passed with no progress at all, except that he had become familiar with local people and the local scene.

He had been accused much of his official life of working

on hunches, and if he preferred to call them intelligent deductions, what did it matter? Hunches came in two kinds: the good and the bad. He had a bad one, now. At some stage in the investigation he had gone wrong. He wasn't yet sure how or where but was beginning to think it was over Caldicott and the Stephensons. Had they been involved he would have expected them to show some kind of panic, but they behaved normally. Caldicott was in his St. John's Wood flat, the Stephensons had gone on from Bath to Cheltenham, visiting picture galleries and antique shops on the way. They were due back in Bath tonight, for a sale next morning.

Should he have picked them up earlier? Should he at least have seen them himself instead of relying on others to tell him what they looked like? And should he see them himself, now? He went into a tiny bathroom which had a shower, not a tub, and began to undress. He was stripped down to his underpants when the telephone bell rang. He turned back, without effort, muscular lean, very flat at the stomach; he had a good body and was proud enough to take good care of it.

"West," he announced.

"Kempton here," the Chief Inspector said. "I think we've found something. At Gorley Woods, sir. A local man is on his way to pick you up."

*   *   *

Gorley Woods was entrancing in the evening light. The sun caught the western branches and gilded the green and spread an eerie glow among the leaves at the top of the trees; and a gentle wind moved light and shadow, leaf and branch. It was high on one of the great stretches on the Plain, at the top of a long climb from Salisbury towards Blandford, surprisingly near the road and yet hidden from it by a cutting in the crest of another hill. A dozen policemen, as many farmers and some newspapermen were gathered about, as well as ten or tweve youthful-looking soldiers. Kempton and Tom Batten stood by a slender tree, young compared with most of the beeches here, while policemen in plain clothes were searching the beech mast and the husks at the foot of the tree itself. New grass spots showed in sparse patches all about the roots which spread evenly from the base of the trunk.

Kempton was on one knee, but stood up when Batten, at the trunk itself, called him. A newspaperman glanced round, saw Roger, and uttered his name; a photographer spun round and his flash went off. Roger reached the tree as Batten said:

"It looks like 'un." He was peering at the trunk at chest height and Kempton was examining the spot just as closely. He took out a magnifying glass and went closer. As Roger drew up, Kempton said to Batten:

"I think you're right."

"About what?" asked Roger.

Both men glanced round, Batten startled, Kempton calmly; and it was Kempton who answered.

"It looks as if Prell was here and fastened to this tree, sir. There are several pieces of linen-strands, I mean. She was wearing a loose-weave linen suit of those colours. Then look down here, sir." He bent down again and Roger knelt beside him. "Do you see the scuff marks on the root of the tree just above the ground? They were almost certainly made by shoes with iron heel-tips."

Such marks were there, obviously they were freshly made. Roger studied the ground nearby. It was dusty close to the tree but fairly damp on the edges, although wind and sun had dried the dirt road from the highway. It seemed clear that someone had been standing here, moving their feet; scuffing the ground. Roger stood up and Batten held out his right hand with three strands of linen; a green, a yellow and a brown.

"The bark's rough just here, sir," he said. "If she was tied to it —" He broke off.

"Can we identify the fabric?" asked Roger.

"I can vouch for the colours," Batten said, "and I *think* there's an identical suit only a smaller size at a shop in town, sir, in Salisbury. It would be easy to check."

"Yes," Roger said. "How did you find the spot?"

"A local estate agent going to Blandford and Dorchester saw a metallic-blue Ford Capri coming off this track on to the main road yesterday, just after lunch-time. Two-thirty or so. He didn't think anything of it until he got back today and heard what had happened. So we searched the area. Two or three people have certainly been moving about just here, and a car was definitely here yesterday afternoon, one or two damp patches of soil show the tyre marks. Firestone F100. Haven't found any other distinguishing marks, but photographs may reveal something." Kempton rubbed his great jaw. "Not much doubt she *was* here, sir, so we'll have to concentrate the search in this area. Of course if she was taken away in the car she might be hundreds of miles away by now."

"Yes." Roger looked at Batten. "Better search the ground nearby. Can we rig up some floodlights?"

"Oh, yes, sir! The army will help out with those." Batten gulped. "Do you expect to find a grave?"

"All I know is that we have to look for one," Roger said gruffly.

He left with Batten, ten minutes afterwards, with the precious linen strands in a small plastic envelope. Batten drove his own small Morris while Roger looked about the almost deserted fields and road with the sun behind them, bringing different and darker shades of green and brown. But he noticed very little, he was concentrating so hard on the problem.

Had he gone wrong?

They reached the police station before he realised how far they had travelled, and went to a small office which was assigned to Roger for the duration of the case. Batten went straight to the telephone while Roger unfastened a large, brown envelope addressed to him. Inside were small cards, each filled out with remarkably fine handwriting which sloped slightly backwards. On each was a name and address, and Roger began to look through them. He found what should have been the top card, which read:

*Notes on known visitors to Leech's
preview of forthcoming sale at the
Hart Hotel*

"Is Mr. Murrow there?" asked Batten into the telephone. "Or Mrs. Murrow?"

There were seventy-one cards, the assessment stated, and forty-five had been identified by Leech as trade visitors or local residents. He had identified Caldicott but not the Stephensons.

"Good evening, Mrs. Murrow," Roger heard. "I'm sorry to worry you . . . Oh. Oh! I'm Tom Batten, of . . . Yes, that's right, that Batten."

All of the local people were reputable, according to a note from Isherwood, who was keeping discreetly in the background most of the time. He had also telephoned the police nearest the houses of those who had come from outside Salisbury, and checked on twenty more. He confirmed Leech's view; and he had got descriptions of six unidentified people and made out cards for them.

"I know it's a nuisance but if you could open the shop just for ten minutes while it's still daylight. . . . You're very good, *very* good. In about ten minutes, then." Batten replaced the receiver and looked up in triumph. "We can see that suit I talked about, sir. That's if you'd care to come."

"Try to keep me away," Roger said.

The shop was on one side of the market square, with windows at three levels. In the street-level window were dresses which looked not unlike Linda Prell's suit, but of different colours. Footsteps sounded inside the shop, and a shrimp of a man with a bald head opened the door.

"Hallo, Mr. Murrow. Very good of you. This is Superintendent West. . . . If we could see the pale blue, green and yellow suit like the one Linda bought the other day. . . . Oh, Saturday! Then this was probably the first time she wore it. . . . Ah!" He almost kow-towed before the suit which the man soon brought to them on a hanger. "If we could just see it in the light. . . . You're very good, Mr. Murrow. . . . Will you give me an expert opinion, now: were these strands taken from a dress like this?" There was a brief pause as Murrow examined the strands. Slowly, he nodded and said: "Yes."

"You think they were." Batten's voice rose in excitement. "Can you let us have the maker's description and the colours and design?"

"No trouble at all," Murrow assured him, beginning to

look both eager and excited. "There's a picture of it in the catalogue, very good as regards to the colours, especially."

He went to a tidy roll-top desk filled with order books and invoices, catalogues and patterns, selected a catalogue and thumbed through it until he came to an illustration of an attractive flowered suit with a high-waisted jacket. Roger studied this, and then turned to Batten and asked:

"Do you have a photograph of Woman Constable Prell?"

"I've several." Batten answered, but for some reason he hesitated. Eventually he drew out his wallet and selected two snapshots and an enlargement of the girl. Obviously these were not official photographs, but Roger made no comment, simply took the enlargement and placed it near the head of the model.

"If we cut that photograph out and paste it over the model, we've a perfect photograph for colour television," he remarked.

"So we have," breathed Batten. "So we have!" He appeared to be recovered from his brief embarrassment. "Do you think we could take three strands from the hem? Thank you."

*   *   *

"Identical," declared a young man who worked in the carpet factory at Wilton, a nearby borough as ancient as Salisbury. He put the strands beneath a microscope in the small laboratory at the police station. "Those strands came from identical bales of cloth, even the dye is identical. You can be absolutely sure, sir."

Roger said warmly: "That's exactly what we needed to know."

"I only hope it helps to find Linda," the young man went on. "No news yet, I suppose?"

"Afraid not," Roger said; and he was surprised how much that truth hurt him.

He arranged for copies of the photograph to be rushed to London, where it should catch the late news bulletins, then returned to his hotel. He had a hurried meal, went on to the borrowed office and telephoned Isherwood as well

as Scotland Yard, prepared a brief statement for the Press
saying that Linda Prell had been in Gorley Woods, added the
description of the suit, sent it up to the Photography Department where they would make prints for circulation to the
newspapers and to police forces, then drove himself to Gorley
Woods. He saw the lights in the sky from several miles off,
and reached some cross-roads where a policeman and two
traffic wardens were on duty under a floodlight rigged up
among the branches of a tree. Roger stopped as an officer
came up to him.

"What's the trouble?" he asked.

"Mostly we can't keep the crowd away," the man answered
resentfully. "There must be a couple of thousand of them
near Gorley Woods, come across country from all directions.
There was a traffic hold-up before we could say snap. If
you want to get through to Blandford, sir, I'd take the
first left, and — " He broke off, backing a pace. "It's Mr.
West, isn't it?"

"And I'd like to go through to Gorley Woods."

"No trouble about getting there but if you take my tip
you'll turn off to the left as soon as you see the first parked
cars. All over the place they are, too close to the road. You
keep going into the field and do a half-circle round the cars,
sir. It'll look as if you're going over some young barley
but if you keep close to the hedge you won't do any harm.
Did you follow that, sir?" he asked anxiously.

"Yes, thanks," Roger said.

He checked the impulse to ask if they had found the
body, drove on, and followed the instructions closely. Once
he was off the road itself the track was very bumpy but soon
he was opposite the main part of the copse and within easy
walking distance. He left his parking light on before locking
the car and walking towards the parked cars and the roadway.
The light was bright by the copse itself and spread far
enough to show couples snuggled down in some cars, others,
quite shameless, lying in the fields. No girl was crying "No,
no, don't!" here.

Had the farmworkers heard Linda Prell?

As he approached the road itself he saw cars parked in
all directions and a crowd thick among the trees. A dozen

or so police were keeping a space cleared and in this space men were digging. The light was eerie; the curious movements of the men and the shadows they made were eerie, too. The gaping spectators were — macabre, grisly, ghoulish. He saw a tiny flame about his head, falling down, and ducked. It went out. Half-ashamed, he realised that there were people up in the trees, and one had lit a cigarette and tossed the match down. His attention once caught, he saw dozens of figures squatting in the trees and looking down at the working men.

Kemptom was here, looking pale in the white lights. He seemed to recognise Roger instinctively, and looked up.

"Hallo, sir."

"Hallo. Anything?"

'No, sir, nothing at all. What we at first thought was a grave was old rubbish someone buried weeks ago. Any news your end, sir?"

"If you can call it news. No other suspects were at the gallery."

"I suppose we ought to have expected that," Kempton said. "It certainly doesn't help, sir."

"There's one thing. Those linen threads certainly came from the woman's suit," Roger remarked.

"I wonder what the hell they did to her," Kempton said in a growling voice. "It's bad enough when one of our chaps runs into trouble, but when it comes to a woman officer —" He broke off. "I'm pretty sure about one angle, sir."

"What?"

"She won't be found in these woods. We've seen all the soft ground where she could have been buried and there's no fresh digging. Most of the place is a tangle of roots. There's so little soft ground we haven't had any luck with identifying car tracks or anything else," Kempton went on, gloomily. "I suppose we'd better keep the search going, though."

"I'm not sure we shouldn't call it off until the morning," answered Roger. He watched men scraping dirt from the foot of the tree where the policewoman had been tied, but he wasn't thinking of that; he was thinking of the Stephensons and Caldicott, and the fact that he wished he had questioned them himself. Suddenly, he asked: "Know how far it is to Bath?"

Kempton's answer came back as quick as thought.

"Forty miles or so, sir. Are you thinking —" He broke off.

"The same thing as you are," Roger said. "According to my last report the Stephensons are still in Bath, at the Pump Hotel. I'll tell these chaps to call a halt to this, then we'll get moving."

He was about to drive off when Batten appeared, triumphantly holding some copies of the catalogue picture with Linda Prell's face superimposed.

"Took them myself, sir, and got a pal of mine to do some prints quickly. Not bad at all, are they?"

"Not bad at all," Roger agreed. "You get some tele-printed for the Yard and tell them I'd like nationwide distribution — Press, television, they'll know. I'll take two with me. Kempton and I are on our way to Bath."

9

Night Call

My God! Roger thought some two hours later, she's beautiful.
He kept his face set as if not at all impressed and looked
at Stephenson; he had a faint feeling of revulsion which he
seldom felt in a man. It was perhaps the very fair hair and
near-albino lashes. The freckles. The unfinished look of his
nose and lips. *Had* he been badly burned and then patched
up by a brilliant plastic surgeon? No, Roger decided, the
mass of freckles would not be there if that were so. But
he had never seen a less suited couple if appearances were
anything to go by.

"This is disgraceful," Sarah Stephenson said coldly. She
had an accent which was neither American nor Canadian; perhaps she was English but had lived on the other side of
the Atlantic for a long time. Her phraseology and her icy
manner were undoubtedly English. "You have no right to
invade our privacy at this hour."

Stephenson grunted: "It's an insult, that's what I call it."

"I'm sorry," Roger said briskly. "I hope you will answer
our questions here, but if you would prefer to get dressed
and come to the police station, I've no objection. We have
more facilities there." He was deliberately aggressive, wanting
to push them as far as he could.

He had an odd suspicion: that the woman approved; there
was a glint of what might be admiration in her eyes. But
that was probably imagination. She had made-up for the
night, had on no powder but only night-cream, yet her

features could stand that. Her quilted dressing-gown, pale blue in colour, brought out the pale grey of her eyes.

"What do you want to know?" asked Stephenson in a sulkly, complaining way.

Roger said sharply: "Inspector. Your notebook at the ready, please. Mr. Stephenson — were you at Leech's picture gallery in Salisbury on Tuesday morning?"

"Sure."

"What time, please?"

"Oh, I guess — well, maybe around half-past nine until half-past ten."

"Why did you go there?"

"What's that? What did you say?" The man both looked and sounded vague.

"I said, why did you go there?"

"To see some paintings, I guess."

"*Why*, Mr. Stephenson?" Roger's voice hardened. There was a limit to how far he could push in this arbitrary manner, but he felt confident so far. Stephenson gave the impression that he didn't even know that he was being pushed. The woman, sitting in a small needlework or nursing chair, was also opposite him, and any admiration she had shown had gone. Her gaze was as icy as her manner.

"I heard there was to be an auction and there might be some bargains."

"Who told you?"

"A friend — an old acquaintance of mine."

"His name, please."

Just for a moment something happened to the man. It was as if his mask of pretending that he did not know what all the fuss was about dropped, and there was a hint of triumph in his eyes as he answered:

"Frank Caldicott."

"C-A-L-D-I-C-O-T-T?"

"Sure, I guess that's how you spell it." The mask was down again; the man's voice even sounded different: diffident.

"Where does Mr. Caldicott live, Mr. Stephenson?"

"At Whiteside Court. Number 27, Whiteside Court, St. John's Wood." Stephenson gave the 'saint' its full pronunciation, did not contract it in the English way. Moreover, it was Caldicott's right address.

"And you just went to the gallery to look?" Roger put a lash of scepticism in his tone.

"Sure, sure," Stephenson muttered, and then he flared up. "Say — what is this? Can't a man go and look at some paintings without being hauled out of bed in the middle of the night? Is it a crime in Merrie England to look at works of art or something?" He made the last word sound like 'sumpun' but his indignation seemed real. "So I went to the Leech Gallery to look at some paintings Frankie told me might be easy to buy. He said he thought there was a genu*ine* Gainsborough and a genu*ine* Turner and boy, if that was true and I could have bought them at a good price that would have been quite a day. Yes, sir, quite a day. But when I got there what do you think?" *Wadderyertink.* "There were so many dealers you couldn't even breathe. Those prices would have hit heaven itself. So we got out. Why, we had so much time on our hands we went to look at the cathedral, and I ain't the world's hottest cathedral buff. No, sir." He glanced at the woman, who hadn't stirred and now showed no expression at all. "Let me tell you something, Superintendent, let me tell you this. If it hadn't been for my wife I wouldn't have put my nose inside that cathedral. Not even my nose. No, sir." He drew back and threw his arms up shoulder high. "Did I commit any crime, Superintendent? You tell me that: did I commit any crime?"

At last, he stopped.

A glint of satisfaction showed in the woman's eyes, as if she felt he had ended on a note of triumph. Kempton, in Roger's view, kept a straight face but obviously felt disappointed. Roger turned away from Stephenson as if acknowledging that his challenge had failed. He glanced at the bedside table, at a man's watch and some coins in neat piles, keys, a pigskin wallet. He saw a thin book lying face downwards, and the title read: *Salisbury Cathedral.* He wondered what page it was open at, edged towards the table and looked again at Stephenson, whose 'did I commit a crime?' still hovered on its ring of indignation.

Roger said coldly: "I don't know."

Stephenson gasped: "You don't know what?" The words came out as if they were whining out of a punctured balloon.

"I have no idea what you did after you left Salisbury," Roger replied coldly.

Stephenson looked at him, mouth agape, speechless. Roger seemed to stumble, and put out a hand to save himself.

The woman said in ice-cold anger: "That is insulting." Roger pushed the bedside table and grabbed at the head of the bed. Money, wallet, keys and book all slid towards the floor. Stephenson was still too dazed to help, no one else was near enough. Roger caught the book but could not save the other things. And a smaller book, in green, fell out; he had seen the book when Batten had taken him round the cathedral; it was called *The Sarum Magna Carta.* Genuinely unsteady, Roger straightened up and dropped onto the bed, putting the books on a pillow. He looked shaken as he stared down at a rug which he had rucked up. For a few moments the scene was like a tableau, all the four standing or sitting absolutely still. Both the woman and Stephenson were glaring at Roger, and the woman's lips seemed to be quivering with rage.

Roger looked up, as if baffled.

"Clumsy oaf; I *am* sorry!" He moved from the bed quickly and bent down to pick up first the wallet, then the coins. Kempton rounded the bed to help him and after a few moments Stephenson joined in too. Sarah stood aloof until the last coin had been picked up and Stephenson had placed the money in little piles — pennies, new halfpennies, two, five and ten pence pieces and some fifty pence pieces. "I *am* sorry," repeated Roger. "All fingers and thumbs today. It's been a rough day. Mr. Stephenson, did you see this woman yesterday?"

He took a photograph from his pocket and held it out, his fingers were deliberately unsteady. It was one of the prints Batten had given him of Linda Prell's face superimposed on the model's face. Stephenson, jolted out of his earlier mood, glanced down. He did not move a muscle of his face, and there was a noticeable pause before he answered:

"Yes. She —"

"A moment, please." Roger became much less aggressive but was still authoritative. He thrust the picture in front of Sarah, who looked down at it, eyes still frosty. Unlike the man, she reacted noticeably; she was startled.

"Yes," she answered.

"Where, please?"

"She was in the gallery yesterday morning."

"That's right, she was," Stephenson remembered. "She was quite a woman."

"Have you seen her since?" asked Roger.

"Since?" echoed Stephenson. "Hell, no."

"Why should he have seen her since?" demanded Sarah. "Isn't it time you told us what —" She broke off, catching her breath, and to Roger she seemed to be over-acting very slightly. "Is that the — the missing policewoman? We heard about her on the radio."

"Policewoman?" echoed Stephenson. "You mean — Jeese! *That* girl."

"She disappeared after leaving the gallery," Roger said. "Are you sure you didn't see her again?"

"What are you insinuating?" demanded Stephenson, in the sharpest voice he had yet used. "That I'd forget a woman like that? Are you crazy?"

"I see what you mean," Roger said, putting the photograph back into his pocket. "She left the gallery just after you, and we haven't seen her since. We hoped you had."

"No, *sir!*" asserted Stephenson.

"What do you think has happened to her?" asked Sarah.

"We don't yet know," Roger said grimly. "We only know that she was in the gallery to take photographs of the people at the preview, and disappeared."

"I only wish I could help," Stephenson said. "I surely do. I didn't see any camera, though."

"I still don't understand why you had to come here about this as late as it is," Sarah said coldly before Roger could comment. "Is there any special reason, Superintendent?"

"We have to catch up with everybody who wasn't identified at the gallery," Roger replied, and then flashed a smile for the first time since he had arrived here. "Forgive me if I've been too brusque, Mr. Stephenson, I'm very pressed for time and worried about that young woman." He paused and then asked a mollified Stephenson: "Can you remember exactly what you did after you left the gallery? And whom you saw. That might help a great deal."

"Why, sure," Stephenson said. "I've got a good memory, there isn't much I forget. Eh, honey?" He told Roger exactly what he had done, omitting only his brief talk with Sarah, and his conversation in Ledbetter's room. He mentioned passers-by, mostly approaching Leech's. He seemed much more in control of himself and anxious to show that he had taken no offence.

It was half-past twelve before Roger and Kempton left.

*　　*　　*

Neither Stephenson nor Sarah spoke for a few moments, just stood staring at each other. At last Stephenson went to the door, took the *Do Not Disturb* sign from the inside handle and opened and hung it outside. No one was in the passage. Stephenson locked the door and went to the window, standing to one side and peering out. The two policemen were crossing the road towards a parked car: Roger's Rover. They got in and the car moved off.

At last, Stephenson said: "I could cut their throats!"

"It's as well you didn't," Sarah remarked drily.

"Next time," Stephenson rasped.

"Do you think they know —" Sarah began.

"They don't know a thing but they may guess plenty," Stephenson answered. "He's got a mind, that West. He wanted to jump us into saying more than we did. You did fine, honey, real fine."

"I don't understand why he came to us," Sarah said.

"Because the woman followed us and someone noticed," answered Stephenson. "And maybe Caldicott made them take notice. But no one can tie us in with Ledbetter and his pal, you don't have to worry. Ledbetter's just a rental car man and who would recognise him down here? We won't hear from the cops any more." He put his arm round Sarah's shoulders and eased the dressing-gown off their pale smoothness. His hands looked repellent against the soft skin.

"Honey, they sure did wake me up. How about helping me to get to sleep tonight?"

She said: "If that's what you want."

For a moment, gown and nightdress on the floor by her feet, she looked like a marble statue. But she did not stay like a statue for long.

*   *   *

Roger went to the Bath police station, which he had visited on his way to the hotel as a courtesy. The senior officer on duty had been called out on a suspected hijacking of a lorry-load of cigarettes, so Roger did not stay. He drove towards Warminster and Salisbury without saying much. Bath itself was deserted but the great terraces of streets on the hills were shown by the clear street lamps, and lights dotted among the trees in and up the side of the valley. Soon they were on the winding road which climbed steadily upwards, making fair speed because the headlights of oncoming cars gave them good warning. They were on a straight stretch when Roger asked:

"Anything strike you as noteworthy, Alan?"

"Well —" Kempton began, but didn't finish.

"Go on."

"Well, you would certainly have made them crack if —" Kempton floundered. "I — er — I suppose the truth is that I didn't quite understand what you were after, sir."

"Alan," Roger said. "That pair is hiding a lot. Whether it's to do with Linda Prell's disappearance I don't know but they are certainly hiding a lot. When I showed the photograph to Stephenson he didn't move a muscle."

"I noticed that," Kempton answered.

"So he was keeping himself under rigid self-control," Roger declared. "The woman did a better job in her way, even though she was a long time realising that the sensible thing was to recognise the girl in the photograph. We shook them badly but they didn't crack." He slowed down for a corner, and then went on: "Did you see the guide book?"

"The one on Salisbury cathedral?"

"Yes."

"Well, they're certainly touring the district," Kempton pointed out. "Aren't they?"

"Obviously. Sarah Stephenson made him go to the cathedral, he says."

"You would be surprised where my wife drags me sometimes," Kempton said, only half-laughing.

"And he took the book to bed with him."

After a pause, Kempton said gruffly: "I see what you mean."

"Spell it out," Roger urged.

"He was apparently very interested although pretending to be uninterested."

"That's my guess too," Roger said. "I would give a lot to know why they were really in Salisbury and why they're staying in the area." He drove on for a few minutes before going on: "I want to see Caldicott in the morning. If I drive straight up to London I can get a few hours' sleep, talk to him and be back in Salisbury by midday. I'll drop you off at the King's Arms, as Salisbury's on a direct road to town. Will that suit you?"

"Just right," Kempton said, and stifled a yawn. Then he said: "She was one in a million, wasn't she?"

"Yes."

"What a woman like that can see in a man like that I can't begin to guess."

"A kind of Beauty and the Beast magnetism could be the answer," Roger remarked. "I've seen it before."

"But he's such a repellent-looking beggar."

"Not all women would think so," Roger said, and went on with a note of laughter: "Of course, there could be another reason: money."

"Money?"

"She wore an engagement ring worth thousands of pounds, that dressing-gown was Italian silk, even her slippers were jewelled. She lives and sleeps in money. A lot of women will overcome repugnance now and again if they have everything else they want. And don't imagine she's always as cold as she looked tonight," Roger said. "I want you to make out a report covering this jaunt by noon tomorrow."

"I'll have it ready," promised Kempton.

At about one-fifteen Roger dropped him at the hotel. A little more than two hours later he drew up outside the house in Bell Street, Chelsea. The street lights were on and here and there lights shone at windows but there was only darkness at his own house. As he put the car in the garage he reflected that when Janet was at home she always left a light on in the hallway; usually the boys did, too. The dark emptiness was somehow disheartening, but it wasn't only that. He wasn't sure that he hadn't made another mistake. There were some cases which one mishandled from the beginning: could this be one of them? He put on lights on his way to the kitchen, and opened the refrigerator door. There was cold milk, three-days-old cold meat, cheese which had been left in the ice-box far too long. Nothing had any flavour except the milk which was so cold it hurt his gullet as he swallowed. He ought to have made tea or coffee. He wasn't prepared to do so now, and went upstairs. Not even deliberate recollection of the conversation with Coppell cheered him. There was something wrong about this case. He simply didn't know what it was yet.

And he would feel uneasy till they knew what had happened to the missing girl.

He went to bed at four o'clock, and woke without knowing what time it was but to broad daylight and the ringing of the telephone by his side. He sat upright and took the receiver off but did not answer until he was comfortable. He thought: they've found the girl's body, and his spirits were as low as when he had gone to bed.

"West here," he said at last.

"Good morning, sir." It was recently promoted Detective Sergeant Venables, the tall ungainly man in the office next to his, a notoriously early riser. "A cable's in from New York and as it's turned eight o'clock I thought I ought to call you."

The bedside clock, Roger now saw, said three minutes past eight. But his heart leapt at the news of the cable coupled with the fact that Venables wouldn't have called unless he had thought the news important.

"What's it say?" asked Roger.

"It was in code, sir, but I've decoded it. It's from Captain Goodison of New York Police Headquarters, and it says:

'Stephenson potentially dangerous stop also contact man for rare art and paintings for some museums and public galleries also suspected of being contact man for secret buyers of stolen treasures'." Venables gave a little cough. "I double-checked the word 'treasures', sir. No doubt it's the right one. *Very* interesting, isn't it?"

"Fascinating!" Roger exclaimed and his high spirits bounded back. "I'm going straight to Frank Caldicott's flat. I take it that's still being watched?"

"Closely," answered Venables. "The man on duty has just been changed, and the report from the night man says that everything was normal during the night. In fact Caldicott didn't go out at all. Will you come straight back here from the visit, sir?"

"Yes," said Roger, and got out of bed as he put down the receiver. Already he was phrasing questions for Caldicott and another cable for Goodison in New York.

10

Nice Chap

CALDICOTT OPENED the door.

Something about him reminded Roger of a bull-dog; he must have animal faces on his mind, for he had a sudden mental picture of Tom Batten. Despite the resemblance, or because of it, there was something pleasant in the face: a solid, good-humoured dependability seemed to emanate from this man.

Caldicott frowned. "Good morning. Who — *Oh!*" He stood to one side, smiling, and huge dimples appeared in his cheeks as his mouth stretched wide. His teeth were big, uneven, very white. "It's Superintendent West, isn't it? All alone?"

"Yes," answered Roger.

"Come in," Caldicott said hospitably. "I'm just having breakfast. I suppose you've been up for hours, but if you'd like to join me —" He led the way to a door on the right which opened into a large, very modern kitchen; on an imitation wooden bar stood bacon and eggs, a frying pan with more bacon in it, and an aroma of frying bacon which almost made Roger's nose twitch. A coffee percolator bubbled. "Take a stool," said Caldicott. "Everything's hot, I could serve bacon and eggs in a jiffy." When Roger hesitated for a split second before saying 'no', the other man lifted two eggs from a moulded carton, pushed the frying pan back onto the gas ring and cracked the eggs as the fat began to sizzle. "We'll have to share the bacon, I cooked all there was. Too much for me to tell the truth." He took a large plate from a rack over the gas stove and placed it on the bar with a knife and fork. Finally, as if with sleight of hand, he took the coffee off the ring and poured two cups. "As my father used to say, you couldn't be served quicker in a cook shop!"

"I certainly couldn't," Roger said, adding in the same breath: "Has Stephenson telephoned you this morning?"

Caldicott held a slicer with which he was going to lift the eggs, and stared at Roger as if in astonishment.

"Good Lord, no! What made you think he might?"

Roger looked at him, smiling, still in a very good humour, and replied: "He called you once the night before last, and once the day before yesterday. The Bath police checked the calls from his hotel."

"Oh," Caldicott said, ruefully. "Police dig deep. The trouble with digging deep is that you can never be sure what you're going to unearth. Do you like your eggs lightly or well-done?"

"Well, please."

Caldicott began to scoop bubbling fat over the two eggs, pushing the bacon to one side mechanically. He pursed his rubbery lips, then shot Roger a wry glance from under his brows.

"Truth will out," he said. "Neil didn't call me, his wife did. In fact he didn't want to admit I existed after the fiasco at Salisbury. I'd told him he might pick up some old masters for a song, instead of which there were so many dealers that he would have had to bid against the big boys in the business. I am not in favour with Neil Stephenson. I would be even less in favour if he knew —" Caldicott finished basting the eggs and then turned out the gas, held the frying pan in one hand and the slice in the other; for a flash it seemed as if the eggs, bacon and fat would hurtle into Roger's face. "Oh, hell! I've fallen for his wife."

Roger stared blankly; half-believing.

"Couldn't help myself," Caldicott went on. "Love at first glimpse, as it were. Nothing's happened yet, and probably never will, but she responds at least by telephone. I never was lucky with women. Now! Two well-done eggs and two rashers of over-cooked bacon coming up. Call me a bloody fool, if you like. I am constantly calling myself one. No one with any sense would ever aim for the moon. I am a con-firmed bachelor of modest means and Stephenson is a millionaire at least. However, human beings are human beings, cats may look at queens, idiots can hope for miracles, five minutes' holding hands with Sarah is far better, for me, than bed with any other woman. And I am not exactly celibate." As he talked he sat at the bar and attacked his breakfast with gusto. "Salt? Toast? Forgive me if in the masculine manner I am crying on your shoulder. It may be hard to understand but there are times when having no one to talk to can be purgatory." He gave one of his broad, lugubrious yet happy-looking smiles. "You didn't know you were coming to rescue a man from purgatory, did you?"

Roger, eating with relish, answered: "No."

"My best thanks."

"My pleasure. Exactly what business do you have with Stephenson?"

"May I ask, why all these questions?"

"Do you need to?" asked Roger, sharper than he had yet been.

"Shouldn't I?" As Caldicott buttered a corner of toast, his eyes rounded. "*Oh*. The missing policewoman."

"Yes."

"Surely you don't think —"

"I think someone who saw her at the Leech Gallery might know what happened to her."

"Oh," Caldicott said. "I see. Damned funny, how the mind works. I saw the show on television last night and someone said something about the gallery but I was at the time busy with no doubt lustful fancies. I'm sorry. You can't think Stephenson —" He forked toast, bacon and eggs, and popped the load into his mouth. "Or, perhaps, me?" he suggested. "Whether you can is academic, whether you do is all that matters. I saw this Prell girl of course — rather coltish, I thought, and very proud of her locket camera." So he had noticed that. "She really shouldn't have been let loose among such a crowd, Mr. West. Are you going to ask me questions or shall I make a statement?"

"Both," Roger said. "And we shall ask everyone who was

in that gallery to do the same. Did you see Miss Prell leave the gallery?"

"On reflection — yes."

"What time?"

"Half-past ten or so, I suppose."

"Did you see her at any time after that?"

"No."

"What did you do afterwards?"

"Ambled about Salisbury, spent an hour in the cathedral, had an early lunch at a pub called the Haunch of Venison, walked to the station and caught the next train back to London. That was twelve-thirty, more or less."

"Did you see the Stephensons again?"

"No."

"When did they —"

"Sarah."

"I don't mean from Bath. I mean when did Stephenson first talk to you about paintings — or business?"

Caldicott considered for a few moments before answering:

"Thursday. And he telephoned me again last Saturday. Yes, Saturday. He caught me just before I left for the Yorkshire match, I live here mostly because I'm within walking distance of Lords and a bus ride from Hampstead Heath, my favourite place for constitutionals. Saturday, then. He gave the name of a mutual friend in New York as introduction, and asked me whether I knew where he might buy some good Victorian or earlier period pictures at a modest price. There's a run on the unknown Victorians in the States at the moment, all you have to do is to prove the date: the artist doesn't matter. So I told him about Salisbury and he asked me if I would meet him at this preview. He was touring in a drive-yourself hired car, and I went down by train. You know what happened from then on."

"Yes," Roger said, and placed his knife and fork neatly together on his empty plate. "That was very good indeed, thanks. Who was the mutual friend?"

"Tito, of Madison Avenue."

"Tito!"

"Not the great Yugoslav leader," Caldicott said, grimacing. "There's no copyright in names. Coffee?" He poured out while talking; he seemed never to stop talking. "I don't know whether you have a file on me at Scotland Yard, Mr. West, and whether you have or not I can no doubt fill in some gaps. I am a runner in high-class art circles. Cursed with laziness, blessed with modest tastes, possessed of a good public-school education and a love of paintings and the visual arts generally, I can indulge most of my tastes by this running. I am a very good judge of paintings but haven't the possessive streak which makes some men want to own as many as they can get their hands on. However, I love travel and enjoy nothing more than going from antique shop to gallery. When I see anything that a particular gallery or a certain individual wants, I report it, and buy if necessary on commission. Am I boring you?"

"You are fascinating me."

"Then I've done my good deed for the day! In the course of these activities which I indulge whenever it takes my fancy, I meet some odd characters. Dishonest dealers, for instance. It is distressing how often I tell someone of a rare opportunity and instead of doing a straight deal as a result, they steal the goods or have them stolen. And friends recommend me, my judgment being impeccable as near as damn it. I've been questioned often enough by you chaps to realise that I am suspected of being on the fringe of crime. Your man Kempton once warned me that one day I would find myself tipped over on to the wrong side of the law, but — well, I never help criminals *knowing* they are criminals. And I never work knowingly with ex-criminals, old lags, or known fences. So, I'll take my chance!"

He drained his third mug of coffee, put it down on the bar, and sat back, one elbow on the bar, big face a-smile. Not a bulldog, Roger thought, rather more like the caricature of a cow which had once been on all the hoardings in Paris; the cow that laughed.

He stopped smiling and showed no sign of being amused when he asked:

"You won't let me down over Stephenson's Sarah, will you? Apart from not wanting to get hurt, I don't want to create any problems for her. I *can* rely on your discretion, can't I?"

After a very short pause, Roger answered: "Yes."

"Thank you," said Caldicott simply. He shrugged, and looked crestfallen. "I know it will probably come to nothing, but they're coming back to London for the weekend and at least I'll be able to see her. *Now!* Enough of my bleeding heart. Is there any way in which I can help you?"

"Yes," Roger answered again. "Write down everything you can remember at the gallery, everything you recall of Police Constable Linda Prell, the names of people you saw, anything which may suggest that any one of the people at the gallery took special notice of the police officer. Sign this statement and I'll have it collected this afternoon. If you'd like one I'll have a photocopy made and sent round to you."

"Oh, I'll need one," said Caldicott feelingly. "Do you realise that this will entail more writing than I normally do in a couple of months?" He raised his hands in mock surrender. "Don't shoot, don't shoot! I'm not complaining."

A few minutes later, Roger said: "I must be off."

"Spare a few minutes to see my den," Caldicott urged.

He took Roger into the room beyond the kitchen. Here the walls were crowded with prints, some bookcases, some small pieces of antique furniture, and some big leather armchairs. The carpet was threadbare. The room had both a comfortable and homely look, the abode of a bachelor with rare taste and discernment.

"If I weren't so lazy I would be a rich man," Caldicott said as they shook hands.

Roger walked away from the Regency house, one of a white painted terrace which had been converted into flats, and saw the Yard man sitting in a car at the far end of the terrace. He did not acknowledge the man but immediately flicked on his own radio-telephone and talked to *Information*.

"Superintendent West speaking ... I want the man watching Frank Caldicott in Whiteside Court moved and a less obvious replacement sent ... Yes, closely watched ... Telephone Salisbury H.Q., Chief Inspector Kempton if he's there, if not Mr. Isherwood or Mr. Batten, to say I will be delayed but should be with them at about two o'clock ... Tell Detective Sergeant Venables that I'll be at my office in about half-an-hour."

He rang off and concentrated on driving; the high wall
of Lords, which was smoke-grimed and out of place with the
game played by 'flannelled fools' made him smile, but his
smile was crooked as he thought of Caldicott. He reached
the Yard in twenty minutes, and saw several newspapermen
outside. Cameras flashed and men called out, all their
questions virtually the same: is there any news of the missing
policewoman?

"None at all," Roger answered.

"Are you here to follow a London angle, Superintendent?"

"I'm here to confer," Roger answered, and went inside the
Broadway entrance and up the central lifts. He met no one
from the C.I.D. until he entered the main hall. The doors
of the Conference Room were open and beyond he saw most
of the top brass of the Metropolitan Force standing about,
smoking, drinking coffee. One or two caught his eye; he
wondered if they had been discussing him, hoped they
wouldn't send for him this morning, and hurried along to
his office. Venables came lumbering in when he rang.

"*One*," Roger said. "Have a messenger call on Caldicott
for a signed statement by between three and half-past, and
send a photocopy back to Caldicott. *Two*, check that the
next watch on Caldicott doesn't stick out like a sore thumb.
Three, cable New York and ask them if they've anything on
Mrs. Stephenson, Christian name Sarah, and don't forget to
thank Captain Goodison for the cable we had this morning.
Four, have a dozen photocopies of that cable made, I want
some for Salisbury. *Five* —"

"I've had some cable copies done, sir," Venables reported.

"Good. *Five*, have Bath —" Roger broke off, frowning,
and then said in a gusty voice: "No, I'll talk to Bath. We
want the Stephensons trailed, want to know where they go
and whom they see. Oh, *six* — how would you like a job
for the weekend?"

"Out on the prowl, sir?" Venables's face lit up.

"Watching the Stephensons, particularly the woman."

"I'd love it, sir!"

"They're coming back to town, and it may be to the hotel
they were last time —"

"The Rubens in Knightsbridge."

"Check with the Rubens. And remember I don't want the Stephensons to know why they're being watched. I do want to know how they're going back to America — by sea or air, which sailing or flight, everything possible, so that if necessary I can alert New York."

"I understand, sir," the younger man assured him.

Roger had every confidence that he did. As the other went into the smaller office, Roger put in a call to the Superintendent of the Somerset Police in Bath. Sometimes one seemed to behave in a cavalier fashion with provincial forces, or one took them for granted. This had very nearly happened with Bath, this time, and he wasn't sure that the mood would be amiable. Soon, a Superintendent Soames was on the line.

"Superintendent, I know we've been taking you for granted —" Roger began.

"If you're worried about ruffling our feathers you needn't be," the other man interrupted. "I had your message and I know what you've got on your hands. We'll help where and how we can." Before Roger could respond, he went on: "So forget it. We've been watching your pair, and they're booked in at the Pump Hotel again tonight. At the moment they're on their way to Bristol, and the Bristol Police will pick up their trail. Don't worry about anything this end, Mr. West. All we hope is that you soon catch the baskets." He paused for a moment and then added: "Found her yet?"

"No," Roger answered, and this time he was able to get a word in. "And when we do it will be because you chaps freed our hands. Thanks. Goodbye."

He rang off, and sat back, but had no time to think clearly before the inter-office telephone bell rang and when he answered it, Coppell said:

"I want to see you for five minutes, Handsome. Stay in your office, will you?"

II

Liaison

A MINUTE could be a long time.

Roger simply waited for two or three to pass, then picked up his case and took out notes he had made since the Salisbury affair had begun. He made such notes whenever he needed to refresh his memory about incidents or aspects of a case, and they not only kept him in tune but they formed a basis for the official report he would have to make. Now, he scanned them closely, made a few extra notes mainly about Caldicott, with another covering the co-operation of the Bath police. He had nearly finished when there was a perfunctory knock at the door, and Coppell came in. The Commander was in a new, dark-brown suit and wearing his Metropolitan Police Force tie; obviously he had dressed in his best for the meeting of V.I.P.s.

"Don't get up," he said, as Roger started to rise. "Mustn't stay, I've got to take a message back to the others." He stared levelly at Roger, who began to suspect there was something wrong, before asking abruptly: "Does it matter where you go? On business, I mean."

Roger said, slowly: "Well, no. Why should it?"

"Your wife *has* been known to protest if you're away too much."

"Oh," Roger said, heavily. "Yes, she has. But I think we're over the hill where that's concerned."

"Thinking won't help. Do you *know*? Because this appointment might take you away from London a lot."

"I'll go wherever the job takes me," Roger assured him.

"Right!" Coppell was obviously pleased and actually clapped his hands resonantly. "There will be some delay, a few weeks or even months, but it's in the bag." He started for the door, only to spin round again and to throw words out. "How's the Salisbury job shaping up?"

"Badly."

"Found her yet?"

"No, sir."

"This one's a slow starter," Coppell said. "It could build up very quickly. Are you satisfied with the way it's going?"

Hesitantly for him, Roger answered: "I'm not sure I'm tackling it the right way, sir, but that could mean there's something about it which I don't understand." He stopped as if in pause, but didn't go on. Coppell, waiting, suddenly moved to a corner of the desk and sat down.

"What's worrying you?" he demanded. "I can see there's something."

Raising his hands, Roger gave a snort of a laugh.

"It could also be that I got such a big lift out of what you told me the other day that I muffed the first job I tackled afterwards. And there's the usual extra sensitivity about the fact that a police officer is missing. Apart from wanting like hell to find her, there's a feeling that the eyes of the police are upon me. Do you see what I mean?"

"When I first took this job I felt —" Coppell began, and then switched what he was going to say: "Have you any positive problems apart from these psychological ones?"

He was being the man he should have been for years: helpful, understanding, not simply demanding results. A few months ago he would have been so obsessed by the meeting of V.I.P.s that he would have been off by now, giving the impression that he didn't want to be troubled. Instead, he waited.

"Motive," Roger said.

"Can't you find one?"

"Not big enough to justify the obvious kidnapping and possible murder of a police officer. Even if someone had planned to steal those pictures, I wouldn't have thought they'd go this far. One possible motive is that Linda Prell heard or saw something that was significant enough for them

to stop her at all costs. I can't believe a plot to steal those
paintings would be big enough. Discussion of a plot to steal
in itself isn't a serious offence. If she'd reported one, all we
could have done was warn the plotters off. So it was something much more significant."

"Possibly they're fakes and this could be part of a major
fraud," Coppell said.

Roger pursed his lips. "It would have to be a damned big
conspiracy."

"And you've no ideas?"

"Nothing specific," Roger admitted. "There are at least
six places within easy reach of Salisbury which would yield
a very big haul. The biggest are Longford Castle and
Wilton House. Each has paintings worth millions as well as
having great sentimental value to the families. I'm going to
suggest a special watch on each of them, but it's not easy to
watch these big houses standing in their own grounds.
There's some priceless stuff in the cathedral, too."

Coppell's lips thrust themselves even further forward.

"Couldn't be thinking of Magna Carta, could you?"

Roger said slowly: "I don't want to."

"Well, I shouldn't," said Coppell decisively. "No buyer
would touch it, they'd have dynamite on their hands." He
stood up. "I must go. Keep at it." As he opened the door,
well ahead of Roger, he barked: "As if you ever stop!" He
went out, letting the door slam, and it was easy to imagine
that the floor of the passage shook.

Roger dropped into his chair.

This Coppell was a pleasure to work with, but that didn't
make him right. Of course, the idea of the theft of Magna
Carta was ludicrous, and yet the book by Stephenson's bed
had been opened at the cathedral with a picture of Magna
Carta on one side. He needed to know more about the
document, where it was kept, how it was secured; on the
other hand he didn't want to alarm the local people or alert
the police and even more particularly, alert the Press.

It was probably a silly idea, anyhow.

There was a tap at the communicating door, and Venables
came in. He had a vague facial resemblance to Caldicott, but
in build he could not be more different; tall, rather clumsy

with big hands and feet. Of all the younger men Roger knew at the Yard Venables was the most promising detective. He was acting as Roger's assistant partly to get training and experience; even his appearance would not long delay promotion to inspector's rank.

"What is it?" Roger asked.

"Have you anything new for the Press, sir?"

"Nothing new," Roger answered. "And all statements will be issued from Salisbury, anyhow. Have you laid everything on?"

"Yes, sir." Venables moistened his lips. "And I can tell you that the Stephensons are due to fly to New York by Transworld Airlines on Sunday afternoon — on a Boeing 747."

"Humph. Doesn't give them much time to pull off any big deal, does it?"

"Not unless it's already in hand, sir."

"About to be pulled off under our noses; is that what you mean?"

"It *is* possible, sir," Venables said, solemn-faced. "Are you leaving for Salisbury soon?"

"Almost at once," Roger told him. "Is there anything you think I ought to do here first?"

"No, sir, but I haven't had a chance to tell you that Detective Sergeant Batten telephoned twice this morning, and once only five minutes ago, I didn't disturb you as the Commander was here. Batten seems very worried indeed, sir. He called from a prepayment box and asked if you could possibly see him unofficially."

Roger frowned. "Not semi-officially?"

"No."

"Did he say what he was worried about?"

"Only that he would very much like your advice on a personal matter. He — er —" Venables hesitated, and moistened his lips again. One of his disadvantages was that he could not control his expression well, and at this moment he had a guilty look which virtually told Roger that he was on the point of a confession. "He was so worried, sir, that I took the liberty of saying you *might* be prepared to meet him on your way into Salisbury. A kind of chance meeting, if you follow me."

"Where?" demanded Roger.

"There is a garage called Cornerways at a fork in the road about ten miles out of Salisbury," Venables answered, brightening. "One road goes to Andover, one to Stockbridge. Coming from Salisbury that is. Apparently he has to make an inquiry there about a stolen car, and he said he would be there around half-past three."

"And what time will I get there if I leave now?" asked Roger.

"About half-past three!" Venables answered, his eyes glowing. "I warned Salisbury you might be late, sir?"

Roger smiled to himself as he left the office: smiled several times on his way out of London; wondered what Batten wanted, then considered whether Batten was the man to talk to about the cathedral and Magna Carta. Obviously Venables had become very well disposed towards the Salisbury man but there was an angle which mustn't be overlooked. Batten did too much off his own bat. He, Roger, had always been sorely tempted to do the same. Some of his earlier clashes with Coppell had been because he had made decisions without consultation, often because he had doubted whether he would get approval. That was one thing: he had always been able to take any consequences personally, and no one had shared that with him. Now if he encouraged Batten on his lone wolfing he might find the man taking this as official approval from Scotland Yard.

He did not know Batten well.

He did know that if he had met the man casually he would have had some doubts of his trustworthiness. One took a policeman's trustworthiness for granted but Batten might be trying to use him for his own advantage. The way he had approached Roger in the first place made it clear that he had wanted Roger involved in the case.

There was the incident of the photographs, too. Batten was a family man; what was he doing with several snapshots of Linda Prell in his wallet? He had admitted to being impulsive as well, a characteristic all policemen had to keep severely in check.

Roger tried to put these thoughts out of his mind, but they kept recurring. He was in Sunningdale, bumping over the level crossing, when another thought drove Batten, Linda Prell and the whole Salisbury affair out of his mind.

What had Coppell really implied by wanting to know whether he, Roger, would object to travelling? Travelling *where*? He was preoccupied by that when he reached the traffic lights at the approach to Camberley. Waiting on the other side of the road was a metallic-blue car with a youthful driver and a dark-haired girl beside him. Such a car had been reported leaving the copse where Linda Prell had been held for a while. The recollection was brief and passing; he had forgotten it by the time he had passed the main entrance to Sandhurst College.

It was half-past two; he was making good time.

*   *   *

At half-past two Linda Prell opened her eyes and looked about her vaguely. She was in a darkened room, gagged and tied hand and foot to a narrow bed. She heard no sound. She had no idea where she was. An overwhelming thirst and a throbbing headache made her feel not only afraid but ill.

When a sound did come, it made her start; she tugged uselessly at the cord binding her wrists.

A door opened and bright daylight shone in, dazzling, actually hurting her eyes. She recognised the man Ledbetter by his voice; all she could see of him was a dark silhouette against the brightness.

"I want to talk to you," he said, without expression, and he leaned forward and unfastened the knot of the scarf which gagged her. Then he stood back, and without the slightest warning demanded in his flat voice: "How long have you and Batten been lovers?"

She gasped: "It — it's not true!"

"Another lie like that, and I'll slit your tongue," he said. "I've been making inquiries and when I get information it's reliable."

Now there was expression in his voice; a lash of savagery. She was sure he knew the truth, it wasn't any use lying. She knew that she couldn't face pain, or greater fear; she had no physical courage left.

She said: "Two years."

"How often does he take you with him on his night tour of the cathedral?" Ledbetter demanded. "Tell me that, and you can have some water."

Water, she thought; how she craved water; she had to have water!

"He — he only took me once," she said. "Just once."

"Does he know how to cut off the security contact with the police station?" Ledbetter demanded. He took a flask from his pocket and unscrewed it, and water suddenly became the most precious thing on earth.

"He — he said he did!" Linda gasped. "But he didn't do anything that night, he didn't go up to the library." She was sobbing, partly because she knew that this was betrayal, and she was too weak to defy this man.

Ledbetter poured water into the cup-cap of the flask and held it to her lips. The water seemed to soak into her tongue and mouth as if they were sponges, and it was a long time before the significance of the man's questions began to dawn on her. Why should he have made such searching enquiries? How had he come to know about her and Batten? Why was he so interested in the library — where Magna Carta was kept?

*   *   *

At half-past two, Caldicott applauded a boundary which came off the edge of a Middlesex batsman's bat. Thirty yards away from him, a police officer with overlong hair and sideburns sat as if intent on the game, while actually watching Caldicott.

At half-past two, the Stephensons left a hotel in Bristol and walked along towards the university buildings, up the steep hill. It was pleasantly warm, and the rented Jaguar, parked in a side street, was very hot. As he opened the door for Sarah he saw a slip of paper on the seat, pushed through a side window which he had left open deliberately for such a message. He picked up the paper as he slid inside, and showed it to Sarah. It read: 871242. He repeated the number to himself several times until he knew he would remember it, and then said:

"I'll be back."

She didn't speak, but watched as he walked to a red telephone booth not far away. Someone was inside it and he had to wait several minutes, pacing up and down. She studied her diamond ring, turning her hand right and left and shooting the scintillations off in all directions. She wore a pale green, printed linen dress without sleeves, natural-coloured stockings and shoes and gloves slightly darker than the dress.

At last, Neil went inside the kiosk. He was there for at least ten minutes. First one, then two other people came out for it and stood about, but he kept his back to them all. When at last he came out his stride, for him, was positively jaunty. He opened the car door and beamed at her, saying:

"Did you know you look del-*licious* today?"

"Yes," she answered. "I knew."

"And delectable," he added, getting in. He ran his hand up and down her bare arm and she didn't flinch or try to move away. "Honey," he said, "I think we're going to have an easy ride."

"Then you're crazier than I thought you were."

"Don't be like that," he protested, squeezing her arm. "There's word from Nicodemus which says he has already got an offer for at least five million dollars."

"Good God!" Sarah exclaimed. "Five million!"

"You see how crazy I am, honey. I'll tell you how crazy. I've had Ledbetter making inquiries through another guy who won't talk, because Ledbetter's got too much on him. And I've got a real expert working with him, a kid named Bryce who's tops in electronics. I haven't wanted you to know before but it's okay now, we won't be long. We had a big piece of luck; our dear little lady guest and the zealous Detective Sergeant Batten are lovers. What do you know? Batten is a man with a wife and three children, carrying on with an unmarried policewoman like that. And Batten's one of the security guards at the cathedral, he knows all the tricks. Didn't I tell you this was going to work out just fine?"

"I'm beginning to think you might be right," Sarah

admitted. Excitement sounded in her voice and shone in her eyes. Stephenson patted her knee, and slowly settled at the wheel. His door wasn't quite shut. As he opened it to slam it, the slip of paper with the number blew out. It fluttered along the pavement towards a big church which stood facing three ways, and it was noticed by a uniformed policeman who had been standing talking to a traffic warden. The policeman walked on, reflecting that the driver of the car was like the man Stephenson he had to report on. The car disappeared and the policeman saw the slip of paper catch against some wallflowers in a small flower bed near the church. He waited until the car was out of sight and he could not be noticed in its driving mirror, before going to the slip of paper which had now been caught in a gust of wind and carried twenty or thirty feet further away. The policeman broke into a run, tried twice in vain to tread on it, and on the third time, kept it under his boot. He bent down and picked it up, reading: 871242. He took out his notebook, placed the paper between the leaves, then took out his walkie-talkie radio.

*   *   *

"Here's something," a Salisbury Information-Room man said to Chief Inspector Kempton, half-an-hour later. "A report from Bristol, sir. One of their chaps on the beat saw a man put a slip of paper into Stephenson's car when it was parked. Stephenson went to a telephone booth as soon as he got back, carrying a slip of paper in his hand. The piece of paper was blown out of the car when he got back and it just had a number on it, reading 871242, which looks like a telephone number."

Kempton rubbed his big chin.

"It could be. Is Bristol checking?"

"I don't know, sir," the local man said.

"Then I'd better ask them to," said Kempton, looking at his big wristwatch. "It's nearly half-past three. Mr. West ought to be here soon. Let's see if we can do a quickie on this job, shall we?"

12

Confessional

TOM BATTEN WAS SITTING in a police car at the corner garage when Roger pulled in for petrol. Roger appeared not to notice him, but after the garage hand had started filling his tank, Batten came up. He was smiling his now familiar smile, and his eyes seemed buried deep in their sockets. Shy? wondered Roger. Trustworthy? There was absolutely no way of telling.

"Hullo, sir," Batten said. "Fancy seeing you here."

"What's brought you?" Roger asked. "Our case?"

"No, sir, I'm afraid not. There's been a report of some stolen cars in the area and I'm doing a quick check. No luck here, though. Have you got five minutes, sir — about 'our' case?"

"Yes," Roger said.

"Move Mr. West's car, Teddy, when you've finished with it," Batten said, and opened Roger's door. "We'll have a cuppa in my car." He did everything so casually that Roger could almost have been persuaded that it was an accidental encounter. There was some kind of telepathy, for a girl from the café brought a tray of tea as they got into the small police car. "Expect you can do with this, sir."

"Yes, thank you," Roger said, and the girl went off. "Sergeant," he said to Batten, "I don't know that I like this kind of surreptitious meeting. I can't promise I shall keep what you have to say to myself."

"I quite understand, sir," Batten said. His eyes were shadowed, there was a curious intensity in him and Roger had no doubt that he was very worried. "The truth is, I don't really know what to do about a personal matter which is a police matter also. I'm in a very difficult position and you, being a stranger to the district like, can see clearer than I. I'll bide by your decision, whatever it be."

Whether he was simply being cunning or was wholly genuine, Roger didn't try to guess. He did know that he was inclined to be sorry for the man, who was certainly in some kind of trouble.

Roger said: "I'll help if I can."

"I know you will, sir. I can talk to you, whereas I can't talk to Mr. Isherwood or any of my own senior officers. I'm a married man, sir, with three children all under ten. Happy enough as marriages go but you know how they go, sir, don't you? Well, to come straight out with it, I'm as worried as hell for two reasons. Linda — Linda Prell and me, well, we had a thing going between us. She being dedicated to her work as a police officer she didn't want to get married, and me having a bit of a roving eye by nature, we got this thing going. And — and I'm fond of Linda, Mr. West. I daresay to a sophisticated man like you it doesn't mean much if a man says he's in love, but that's what it amounts to, sir. Linda's come to mean a lot more to me than fun in bed. A lot more."

Roger said, heavily: "This business must hurt like the devil."

"Not knowing whether she's alive or dead or what happened to her or what might be happening, it's awful. I can hardly concentrate." Batten's voice was hoarse. "Oh, I can pull myself together when I have to, it hasn't stopped me working properly, and I've a personal reason for wanting to find her. So I've an extra incentive, you see. But — what if it comes out, sir? The newspaper people are always asking questions and these Fleet Street chaps are different from the local ones. They don't care what they ask."

"Have they been at you about this?"

"Not at me, sir. But they keep asking about Linda. Why, there's one man from the *Daily Call* who's actually asked whether she had any other reason for disappearing, whether it's a hoax, so to speak. And some have been asking if Linda had a lover."

"Who have they asked?" demanded Roger.

Sympathy took away the edge of anger but anger was there because such a situation had existed without his being told at once. If a newspaper broke this story it could have smashed on his head without the slightest warning. The relationship between this man and the woman in his life wasn't a police issue but the behaviour of police officers was; both of them had laid themselves open to blackmail.

There was also the human element, so very real and painful; this man was in anguish.

And there was the police angle, cold and relentless.

"Linda lives with her married sister, sir, and her sister and brother-in-law know the situation. They're very broadminded, and they've an extra room at their flat. It's in a converted house, rather secluded, you know the one — I pointed out a Mr. Withers, didn't I? He owns the place. And did I point out Stephenson?" Batten sat further back than he had been and nearly knocked over the tea. "My dear God," he exclaimed, "what's happening to me? I can't even remember straight!"

"Why should you think I might be interested in Stephenson?" asked Roger.

"Only because he'd been with Caldicott a lot," answered Batten.

"Who else have these newspapermen approached?" demanded Roger.

"Two — two or three of the neighbours, sir."

"At the flats?"

"Yes. The tenants told Meg — that's Linda's sister, sir."

"Have the newsmen asked any policemen?"

"If they have no one's told me," replied Batten.

"Do any of your police colleagues know?"

"I can't be absolutely sure, sir, but I don't think so. I've never confided in anyone and I'm sure Linda hasn't either. A few of them might have an idea but I don't think they know for certain. Linda and I have never — never let on at the station, none of this touching hands business. We've always been very matter-of-fact. Good friends, you know,

8—TTOMC * *

but there's a lot of good friendship at the station. I would have said that no one knew, but after this, well, I can't be sure." Batten spread his hands, and went on in a hoarse voice: "What am I going to do, sir? Tell Mr. Isherwood? It's — it's a bloody hard thing to do, but I'm not worried about that so much. I just can't see straight and I don't know the best course."

Roger said quietly: "I think Mr. Isherwood must be told."

Batten gulped. "I dare say you're right, sir."

"Like me to tell him?"

"*Would* you, sir?" For the first time since this discussion had started Batten actually brightened up. "If — if only you would! I know I've no right to involve you, but —"

"This wouldn't be involving me," Roger said. "I can say that you made a remark which made me wonder what was going on and I forced the story out of you."

Batten passed his hand across his eyes and muttered: "Thank you, sir." After a pause which seemed to last for ages, he went on: "What — what do you think I ought to do, sir? Leave the case?"

"It isn't a decision for you or me," Roger said. He watched the man who had become wizened and old-looking, and felt the warming of compassion: so, he went on: "I know what I would do."

"What's that, sir?" Batten was eager.

"I'd put you on the case full-time," Roger said. "I'd keep you so busy you'd have no time to worry. And I'd tell you to answer any questions the Press put to you."

"About us being *lovers*, sir?"

"About you being good friends. What about your wife in all this?"

"Well," Batten said, chokily. "Well, I don't really think she would worry all that much for her own sake. I think — well, she probably knows there's someone, but so long as I keep the home going and don't start throwing any money about on bits of skirt it would not worry her. The scandal might, though, and she'd be in a bad way if she thought it would hurt the kids."

"Tom," Roger said gently, "obviously there's a risk that

this story will break. You're quite right about London newspapermen, they can be ruthless, and in this case they
wouldn't be doing their job properly if they said nothing
once they had proof. You should tell your wife; I feel quite
sure about that."

Batten didn't speak.

"And I'll tell Mr. Isherwood as soon as we're in Salisbury,"
Roger went on. "It's time we got a move on."

"Yes, I know," Batten said. "I shouldn't have worried you
about it. My God, I didn't think anything like this would
happen! When I gave Linda that locket with the camera in
it —it's a Japanese mini-camera, wonderful little job — I
thought she'd find it useful. It was a birthday present, sir. She
can't wait for the day when she's promoted to sergeant, sir,
she —"

Batten broke off, with a catch in his breath.

Roger could almost hear him saying to himself: but
supposing she's dead!

His car was standing close to Batten's, and he drove off
first, troubled but not yet worried that the man might do
something drastic, such as take his own life. Yet there was
anguish in his mind and he had a terrible battery of censure
to face: letting Isherwood know, telling his wife, facing the
critical comments of his colleagues and friends; facing headlines. Roger pulled into the side of the road a few miles up,
and waited. Soon the pale blue police car appeared, and he
started off again; there seemed no immediate crisis.

Twenty minutes later, at half-past four, he entered the
police station. He had a feeling that the men at the desk
and who moved about the hall and passages looked at him
with sharper attention than they had, but he couldn't be sure.
The door of 'his' room was open and Kempton was there
with a copy of the London *Evening Standard* spread over the
desk. He looked up, and sprang to attention.

"Glad to see you back, sir."

"Thanks. What's going on?"

"This," Kempton said, twisting the paper round so that
Roger could see the headlines. They spread right across the
paper in a two-line banner which no one could fail to read

yards away. And they told Batten's story in the way he had feared most:

MISSING POLICEWOMAN'S SECRET LOVER

"How about that for a turn-up for the book?" Kempton demanded. "Isherwood's nearly apoplectic over it. Won't talk to the Press or do or say a thing until he can discuss it with you. Sorry to throw this at you the moment you get back, sir. Would you like some tea or something before you go and see him?"

"No," answered Roger thoughtfully. "But I'd like to freshen up. Check that he'll be free in ten minutes, will you?"

It was a minute or two longer than that before he tapped at the door of the Chief Inspector's office, and went in. Isherwood was putting down the receiver. He was pale and for a moment tight-lipped; obviously something had hit him very hard. Roger was suddenly aware of the great variety of pressures to which the headline could subject this man, whose dark hair was brushed back from his forehead which was white and smooth as a billiard ball. His black moustache was trimmed so neatly that it might almost have been false. On his desk was a copy of the *Evening Standard*, opened out so that the front and the back page showed. As he beckoned, his telephone bell rang, and he motioned to a chair and growled:

"Have you seen that bloody thing?" He picked up the receiver as Roger nodded, and rasped: "Inspector Isherwood ... No, I haven't." He banged down the receiver and glared at Roger. "That was the fifth call I've had from a national newspaper to ask if I had any comment. The Chief Constable has —" He broke off. "Oh, hell. Why should I let off steam with you?"

"You have to growl at someone," Roger said mildly. "Did you know about this romance?"

"No. None of my business, anyhow."

"You mean, private lives."

"Yes."

Roger said: "I don't know, Jack. I really don't know."

"Can you stand there and tell me that none of your officers has ever slept with a woman other than his wife?"

"No, of course not."

"Do you ask around to find out what they've been up to?"

"No."

"What the hell, then?"

Roger said ruefully: "If one of our men gets involved with a woman and it affects his work I have to take notice. And there's a lot of temptation in London."

"No doubt," Isherwood growled. "And in Manchester, where I came from, and in Salisbury if it comes to that. I had a woman sitting in that chair you're afraid to put your fanny on, offering me bed and massage as often as I liked if only I wouldn't charge her husband with embezzlement. Bloody attractive woman, too. Don't talk to me about temptation! Every possible way to prevent a copper doing his job is thrown at us yokels as well as you sophisticated coppers in the great metropolis!"

Roger sat down and grinned.

Isherwood glared for a few seconds, and then slowly relaxed.

"Oh, bloody hell," he growled. But he looked better and his colour was more normal.

"Now I know what it feels like to be a sergeant," Roger said. "Jack —"

"I shouldn't have —"

"Jack, do you know who her lover was?"

"No, and I don't bloody well —" He broke off. "No," he repeated, and looked very tense. "Do you?"

"Yes."

"Who?"

"Tom Batten."

Isherwood seemed to freeze. The blood drained from his face again. He put a hand on his desk as if he needed to steady himself. He didn't speak for a long time. The telephone bell rang suddenly, despairingly, but although he started involuntarily, he didn't seem to hear it. Roger leaned forward and lifted the receiver.

"Mr. Isherwood's office," he said gruffly.

"Mr. West? Mr. Kempton wonders if you can spare him —"

"I'll call him back," Roger said, and put the receiver down. He was watching Isherwood who seemed to be about to faint. The silence dropped again broken only by Isherwood's heavy breathing.

At last, Isherwood said in a husky voice: "And it was right under my nose. If the newspapers get hold of this, my job's gone for a burton. You can be sure of that." He lowered himself to his chair. There was a fringe of perspiration on his forehead; a myriad of tiny beads. He eased his stiffly starched collar, still looking at Roger, and seemed to gain fresh strength as he asked:

"Sure?"

"On his personal statement."

"My God!" Isherwood said. And then he added a phrase which lifted Roger's heart to a height he wouldn't have thought possible at that moment. "Poor old Tom." Then he went on in a voice which was hardly audible: "I bloody well ought to lose my job, too, if he could talk to you and not to me. Bloody hell! What kind of a copper am I?"

13

Whisper

ROGER SIMPLY SAT BACK and waited; there was nothing more he could usefully do and say, but he still felt deep satisfaction at this man's attitude. Where both he and Batten were concerned there had been moments of self-revelation, and each man would be better for it.

Isherwood bent down to a cupboard in his desk.

"It's early," he said, "but I never needed a whisky and soda more. And you?"

It would be churlish, and might be hurtful to refuse.

"A tot and a splash," Roger accepted. Soon, each man sat with a glass at his lips, sipping. Roger was more glad of it than he had expected.

"Will you tell me all you know?" Isherwood asked.

"Yes, of course." Roger told the story economically. Time was passing all too quickly and circumstances might soon become pressing. There was Kempton's call to return and there might be a lot in from the Yard. He tried to explain Batten's feelings but he did not have to plead for the sergeant; Isherwood had proved himself above all else a human being.

But the policeman wasn't far behind, for he said: "Should I take Batten off the job?"

"I'd sooner put him on it full-time."

"Will you work with him?"

"Of course," Roger said. "I'm going to leave Kempton here part of the time. I shall go to and fro."

"Suit yourself." Isherwood closed his eyes for a moment

before going on: "One thing's certain. This isn't the time for me to say much to Tom."

"No," Roger said. "Except —"

"What?"

"Let him know that if he helps to find Linda Prell, he's earned himself a kind of reprieve."

"Could do. Handsome —"

The use of his nickname told Roger how he was regarded by this man.

"Yes?"

"What's going to happen if the Press finds out?"

"They're going to use the story."

"Can't we stop —"

"Shouldn't even try," Roger interrupted. "I don't think you would if it came to the point."

"Shall I admit that I know?" Isherwood wondered aloud.

After a pause, Roger answered: "No, I don't think so. Not to the Press, anyhow. You need time to think about this."

"I certainly do! And to think instead of react."

"There's one danger," Roger observed.

"What in particular?"

"That this Batten/Linda Prell situation becomes so important that it supersedes the real problem: whether Linda is alive or dead."

"I know what you mean," said Isherwood. "You needn't worry about that."

"Not where you're concerned perhaps, but where I'm concerned," Roger said. "I nearly forgot to ask you what I wanted to know when I came in."

Isherwood finished his drink and laughed, more natural than at any time since Roger had come in. The perspiration had smeared, and he dabbed his forehead with a snow-white handkerchief as he settled back in his chair. He gave the impression that he was on top of himself; that shock following an angry reaction to the headlines was subsiding.

"Well," he asked, "what did you want to know?"

"Whether you can imagine why Linda Prell was kidnapped?" Roger asked.

"No," said Isherwood. "It's puzzled me from the beginning. The stuff in Leech's gallery was worth three hundred thousand pounds, as it proves, but all in bits and pieces. Anyone planning to steal that would be art thieves in a big way and they would want safety at all costs, they wouldn't be likely to take risks with a police officer unless she had heard or seen enough to put them inside for a very long stretch. Or she could have stumbled on to something sinister. All of which is guesswork," Isherwood added impatiently. "Have *you* any idea?"

"Even we Yard chaps have our pride," Roger observed.

Isherwood frowned. "I don't follow."

"We hate being laughed at."

"Oh, I see! All right, I won't laugh very hard."

"Nice of you," murmured Roger. "What in Salisbury is really big enough to steal?"

"Local family art treasures apart, you mean?"

"Yes."

Isherwood frowned, pondered, wiped his forehead and his neck again, drained the glass to its last dregs — there really wasn't anything there — and then answered:

"Stonehenge? Or the cathedral?"

Roger himself wanted to laugh but controlled the impulse.

"Getting warm," he remarked.

"You can't be serious!"

"I'm very serious."

"My *God*!" choked Isherwood. "You don't mean — you can't mean the Sarum Magna Carta?"

"Don't I?" asked Roger. "Can't I?"

He had expected a startled reaction and even some ridicule although he was sure Isherwood would try to stifle that. He certainly hadn't expected the frown which settled on the other's face; or the parallel lines of a groove which appeared between his eyes. Isherwood did not regard this possibility as ludicrous at all. In fact it brought something to his mind: a new anxiety. He was obviously pondering this deeply before making any pronouncement, but he spoke at last in a very low-pitched voice:

"Do you know that Tom Batten is one of the honorary guardians of the Salisbury Magna Carta? A kind of voluntary unpaid security officer. And there are other treasures in the cathedral library. Linda Prell must know this. Could they want to question her about Batten? Or —" He broke off, and when he spoke again his voice was pitched keys higher. "My God, Handsome: what have we run into?"

The room fell very quiet again. Isherwood was appalled and not even remotely sceptical. It was almost possible to see the thoughts chasing one another through his mind. Before he spoke, however, and before Roger moved, the telephone bell rang again. Isherwood lifted it and barked:

"Inspector's office . . . *Who?* . . . Oh, yes! For you," he said to Roger, and held out the instrument as if he were afraid it would bite him.

Roger stood up at the corner and said: "West."

"It's a call from New York for you, Mr. West. A person to person call, the overseas operator said. Mr. Kempton said I should put it through to you."

"Quite right," said Roger. Who could this be but Ivan Goodison, old friend, old colleague? An American voice sounded a long way off, followed by Goodison's. He had a particularly controlled voice, unmistakably but not aggressively from New York.

"Hello! Ivan?" He pronounced the name more like 'Ee-fan'.

"Hi, Roger!" the other man said. "Good to hear you, fella."

"Very good to hear you. How is Rose?"

"Rose is the greatest," the American answered. "Just the greatest. Roger, what have you run into over there?"

"I wish I knew," replied Roger. "What can you tell me?"

"About the Stephensons, plenty," answered Goodison. "Most of it was in my cable, but I've collected some more from a squeal."

"I can't wait," Roger said.

"Neil Stephenson is scouting for Nicodemus," went on Goodison, "and Nicodemus is —" He paused as if anxious to be sober for the sake of emphasis, and then said: "Nicodemus is a kind of group name for the biggest receivers of stolen art treasures in America. If you're interested, the name stuck when we pulled in an art thief and asked him who bought his stuff. 'Old Nick,' he answered, and it became a joke but it isn't a joke any more. We aren't absolutely sure there's a group of fences, or just one who uses a lot of scouts and leg-men. We've never proved it but we've often wondered whether Neil Stephenson is Old Nick — or Nicodemus himself. It's a sure thing he buys for the big undercover boys from coast to coast. He goes to the limit for anything rare and unusual, and buys for collectors who are satisfied to own a treasure without telling the world. And Roger — one more thing."

There had to be something else; and it had to be significant or Goodison would not have called and would not have talked like this.

"Yes?" Roger said tautly.

"Old Nick has been known to pay five million dollars for some pieces of fine art. And *that's* money."

"That certainly sounds like money," Roger agreed tensely. "How do you know this?"

"You know the way it is. You get enough evidence to convince yourself but not enough to stand up in court. You can take it from me the information is good. Have you any idea if anything in this case could be worth that money?"

"Not over the telephone," Roger replied drily.

"So you do have an idea!"

"I think so," Roger said, and then he asked, slowly: "Ivan, do you know any contact Stephenson has in England?"

"Only the man Caldicott you told me about."

"No one else at all?"

"No," Goodison answered. "Not for certain. I can tell you this about him. He always works through a third party. He uses good operatives and pays them well. He never touches anything hot long enough to get himself burnt. He has a major contact there, be sure of that — someone who will do the dirty work for him. But as for who it is, your guess is as good as mine."

"Ivan," Roger said, "your cable called him potentially dangerous. Is he a killer?"

"Known killers have worked for him," Goodison answered, and for the first time since the call had come through there was a momentary lull. Goodison broke it with a laconic: "He has a weakness, Roger."

"What weakness?"

"Women."

"Do you know anything about his wife Sarah?"

Goodison snorted, before saying with derision: "Wife, nothing! They're not married, she's the latest in a long line. I'm trying to find out more about her, and I'll call you again or else cable if I have any news. Good luck, Roger!"

"I'll need it," Roger said, with feeling.

"Do you remember a time when you didn't get just enough?" Goodison asked, and rang off.

Roger put his receiver down slowly. Isherwood, who had been making notes and reading papers and glancing up at Roger from time to time, now sat back expectantly. Roger said: "Give me a moment, will you?" and sat on a corner of the desk. Goodison had said a great deal and he had made no notes. He took a pencil from his pocket and a slip of paper from Isherwood's desk and made notes of the main factors:

1. Stephenson was working with a man or a group known to have paid up to five million dollars for rare works of art.

2. Nicodemus, either a buyer or a group of buyers for collectors who did not object to buying stolen goods and keeping them hidden.

3. Stephenson was known to have employed killers.

4. His 'Sarah' wasn't his wife, and women are his weakness.

5. His only *known* contact in England was Caldicott but there might well be another.

6. The Stephensons were due to fly TWA 747 to New York on Sunday afternoon.

He turned the notes round and showed them to Isherwood, who scanned them and when he had finished, said simply:

"Five million dollars."

"Only one thing here is worth it," Roger said.

"I'm beginning to feel you're right," Isherwood said tensely. "But they can't get it."

Roger said: "No," with conviction.

"Of course they can't get it!" Isherwood repeated roughly.

"The whole idea is preposterous! Even if we hadn't been warned they couldn't get at Magna Carta. And we have been warned, so there's no danger at all. What are we worrying about?"

"I know exactly what you mean," Roger said, and after a long while, stood up slowly and folded the sheet of paper with his notes on and thrust it into the inside pocket of his jacket. "Jack —"

"We haven't a thing to worry about," Isherwood asserted doggedly.

"Except Linda Prell."

"Good God, man, you can't measure a national heritage like that against a life. You know that as well as I do."

"You can't," Roger said. "I can't. Perhaps some people can."

"I don't understand you," Isherwood growled. "We know the Sarum Magna Carta's in danger. All right, correction, we think it's in danger. So we can protect it. Why, if I thought there was any danger at all I'd ask the Army to surround the cathedral! And they would in no time at all."

"Jack," Roger said, "Stephenson represents this Nicodemus, who is an individual or a syndicate. Nicodemus buys very heavily in the stolen fine art and similar markets. Don't you see what we've got here?" When Isherwood didn't answer he went on: "We could catch an enormous bag of big fish if —"

"If we take a chance with the Magna Carta?" interrupted Isherwood. "That's bloody sacrilege."

"Whatever it is and whatever we do, let's keep the name of Magna Carta out of everything," Roger suggested. "Let's just see how things go. We're warned, as you say. We can take quick action if we have to." When Isherwood seemed only to glower at him, he added: "This could be a chance in a million of getting that big haul."

Isherwood growled: "I'll sleep on it."

"Fine," said Roger. "So will I. Will you see Tom Batten?" He put the question so quickly that it seemed to take Isherwood by surprise, but at last the Salisbury man nodded and said:

"Soon."

"I'm very glad I came down here," Roger said.

He went out. For a reason he couldn't understand he felt both weak and very much alone. That was nonsensical, but a fact. He felt *alone*. He felt as if he faced a great challenge which had emerged out of nothing. A rather hoarse West Country voice came out of the blue on the telephone and here he was, suddenly thrust into the cauldron of the nation's history. He knew exactly what Isherwood meant by saying: "That's bloody sacrilege." He walked slowly towards a window at the end of the passage, passing the open door of his own office. He saw a movement and heard Kempton call: "Sir!" but he didn't stop, just went on to the window. It had a view of the western part of the city and, about a mile away, of that incredible spire. He had first seen it perhaps thirty years ago and remembered it for years as the most impressive building he had ever seen. He could hear the voice of a deacon who had shown him and a small party of youngsters round.

"The main building took about eighty years to build. There is no estimate of the cost, but we know it was the dedicated work of hundreds of monks and laymen. The first abbot who conceived the building saw the completion of the main cathedral but about fifty years later his successor made the extraordinary decision to build the spire on to the squat tower."

Now, the spire seemed to guard the city and all the countryside around.

And it guarded its treasures.

And it guarded the Sarum Magna Carta, one of the four surviving.

He thought, with a strange constriction in his throat, of the purpose of Magna Carta. Of the power of the king and the poverty of the people and the restriction on the rights of the nobility. Of the gathering of the barons and the rumbles of revolt until at last the king was compelled to sign, or at least to place his seal.

It was as if the barons were here at this very minute, riding winged horses across the sky to join in the invisible forces which were already gathered and the new forces which would gather soon to protect the ancient charter of the people's rights. He could remember one paragraph as if it were in front of him now.

We will appoint as justices, constables, sheriffs, or other officials only men who know the law of the realm and are minded to keep it well.

Keep it well; keep it well; keep it well.

He heard a rustle, behind him. He knew with one part of his mind who it was and that he should turn and talk to him, but he was held by that vision which was not truly a vision of the barons riding to the king.

"Sir." It was Kempton, patiently.

"Yes," Roger said. "I'll be with you in a moment."

"I think it's very urgent," Kempton said.

"Yes," said Roger. "All right. What is it?" He turned round, was aware of the intensity of Kempton's expression and of the man's surprise when he saw Roger's face.

Kempton held a slip of paper in his hand.

"I think this is the telephone number which Stephenson called from Bristol today," Kempton said. "I'm sure it is." He held out the slip which said in his own bold black hand: 871242. "I've had the Yard working on it, and they have just traced it — decoded it, in fact. It's a local number: Bodenham — BOD — 249. And it's the number of a Mr. John Withers, who lives at Newall Lodge, Bodenham. He occupies the main house, and Linda Prell's sister lives in a flat in the Old Stables in the same grounds."

14

871242

ON THAT INSTANT Roger wondered whether Kempton had any idea of the Batten *affaire* with Linda Prell. Then he judged from the expression on Kempton's bovine face that nothing beyond the simple facts lay in this man's mind. And the facts were significant enough; Stephenson had telephoned the man Withers from Bristol; or else, someone at Withers's number. Roger, back towards the window and the spire, still feeling shaken by the near-psychic experience, walked towards his office. An inconsequential thought passed through his mind: that there was something very dull, or at least unimaginative about Kempton, who didn't improve on acquaintance in the way that Isherwood did.

He rounded his desk and sat down.

"Is this what you tried to tell me about earlier?"

"No." Kempton looked at him as if puzzled. "That was to tell you that Captain Goodison was going to call you from New York. Did he have anything useful to say, sir?"

Roger handed him the notes, and stared at the numerals 871242 as Kempton read what he himself had jotted down. Here was a completely new slant: that Stephenson, who was supposed to have met Withers by chance in Salisbury, had telephoned him or someone at his number furtively, from Bristol. Withers? Or a servant? He needed to find out quickly.

Kempton put the paper down and breathed. "What could be worth five million dollars?"

"That's what we have to find out," Roger said. "Have you done anything at all about this number?"

"No," answered Kempton. "But I was out at Newall Lodge this morning because the missing woman lived in a flat there. It's quite a place, sir."

"Did you see Withers?"

"No," answered Kempton again. "But I had a report on him and the house prepared by a local — village — constable. I always like to know where I'm going." Yes: he would be very thorough. "A copy is in your file."

"Good," Roger said, and then pondered and added slowly: "I think I'll call Mr. Withers and go and have a word with him." He stretched out his hand for the telephone and asked for Bodenham 249; a moment later the operator said:

"It's engaged, sir. I'll call you back."

Roger replaced the receiver, and on the spur of the moment he asked: "How far is it to Bodenham?"

"Not much more than ten minutes' drive," answered Kempton. "Thinking of going out there?"

"I'd like to see what the place is like," Roger agreed. "Anything to keep you here?"

"No, sir." Kempton was eager to show how well he had come to know the district.

He succeeded in impressing Roger by going through the back streets of the city offering a magnificent view of the cathedral which he hadn't seen before, then taking him through the close itself. Hundreds of people were on the great lawns, crowds were thick at the main doors of the cathedral. Traffic was held up by a throng of young clergy standing by the side of a blue coach. A very tall cleric with a high-bridged nose was speaking to this group. He had a clear, carrying, resonant voice.

The driver of the coach pushed the crowd back for the police car and several behind it to pass.

"Can't expect them to hurry for us," Kempton said ruefully, "but we really won't be long now, sir."

They passed through an ancient arched gateway into a narrow street, then on to a roundabout and a main road. Kempton put on speed, blurring the view of beech trees and

9—TTOMC * *

green countryside, until he slowed down to turn off on to a winding road.

"Practically there now, sir. See that white cottage? It's at the entrance to Newall Lodge."

The cottage had a border of flowers, and soon, as the wheels crunched on pale gravel, lawns and hedges came into sight. Kempton stopped at a fork in the drive, and pointed at an old building with a clock tower, on the left. In front of the building was a close-cut lawn, and around this widely-spaced bushes.

"That's Stable House, sir — the old stables now converted into flats. Batten's sister lives in one of those — oh, damn!"

"What's the matter?" Roger asked.

"Car just coming up behind," said Kempton. "I've come too far past the fork to go back."

He slipped the car into gear, and went up the steep drive. As Roger saw the parkland opening out in front of him, he actually forgot why he was here. The house itself, of red brick, looked neo-Georgian; but the great trees, the lawns, here and there splashes of colour from small flower-beds, had a breathtaking effect.

"It's Withers," Kempton announced, as he pulled up close to one side of the house, nose close to a tall window through which Roger could see desks and books.

The other car, a cream-coloured Rover, pulled up alongside, and Withers got out. Roger noticed that he limped a little. The tanned face was startlingly young against a lot of rather untidy silver-white hair. He held Roger's door open, and smiled pleasantly.

"Good evening, Superintendent! You couldn't have chosen a better evening for Newall Lodge."

"The trees are magnificent," Roger said, awed.

"I'm glad you think so," responded Withers. "They really made me buy the place! Would you care to walk round while we talk? Or must our interview be inside?" There was a hint of laughter in his voice.

"I'll gladly walk," Roger said.

He ranged himself on one side of Withers, Kempton on the other, and there began one of the oddest interrogations Roger had ever conducted. When he asked a question Withers answered promptly, but into every pause he interposed some remark about the trees.

"Do you know a Mr. Caldicott, who —"

"I met a Mr. Caldicott in the bar of the Rose and Briar a night or two ago. He was with the Stephensons. That was the first time I saw him. *Isn't* that cedar of Lebanon perfect?" He pointed to a huge tree in one corner, the branches of which swept the ground.

"Magnificent. Do you know Stephenson?" asked Roger.

"Hardly at all. But I'd like to get to know his wife better!"

"Has he ever been out here?" asked Roger.

"Once, two mornings ago. To look at my paintings. I'm sure you didn't come just to ask the questions Chief Inspector Kempton asked earlier!" Withers was now smiling broadly.

"I came because Mr. Kempton told me what a wonderful home you have, and I like to familiarise myself with the place I'm working in." He met Withers's startled gaze with a disarming smile. "That *can't* be a Douglas fir."

He pointed, absorbed in the trees, and caught his foot in a rut in the grass; he would have fallen but for Withers's quick support. The rut was one of two which ran parallel, and Withers said apologetically:

"My gardener hasn't quite got the hang of a big new mower and cutter, I'm afraid. Are you all right? Didn't hurt yourself?"

He was almost too solicitous, Roger thought, as he tested his ankle and replied reassuringly:

"I'm fine, thanks. *Is* that a Douglas fir?"

"Yes — and believe it or not, it has three trunks," Withers replied. "Come and have a look, Superintendent."

The tree did in fact have what seemed to be three trunks growing straight out of the ground as well as a dozen branches which actually grew into the ground; it was dark and shadowy beneath the higher branches, like an enormous tree house.

Question followed question; answer followed answer; and item after item of information about trees native to a dozen foreign lands followed one another. They walked close by a walled garden of warm red brick, then up the drive towards the house again.

"I hope you've time for a drink," Withers offered, when they were back at the front drive. Roger avoided a patch of white on the gravel close to Kempton's borrowed car as he looked at a flower bed which positively blazed with colour.

"I only wish we had," he said. "I've spent too much time here already, sir — and wasted too much of yours."

"Oh, nonsense!" Withers replied lightly. "I love showing off these grounds."

It was obvious that he did.

On the way back to Salisbury, Roger said little and Kempton only answered questions. There was a sense of anti-climax as they drove along the road by which they had come. The coach had gone from the close and fewer people were about, but the sun shining straight on to the west door tinged the grey stone with gold; and glory.

They went back to Roger's office, and Roger seemed hardly to have had time to look at Kempton's notes on Newall Lodge when the telephone bell rang. Roger lifted the receiver.

"A call from Detective Sergeant Venables, of New Scotland Yard," the operator said.

"Put him through."

"Here he is —" the operator began, but Venables's voice was suddenly imposed over it, obviously it was an excited Venables.

One thing was certain: he seldom got excited, and whenever he did it was with a very good reason. Roger's thoughts were wrenched away from Withers and his trees.

"Mr. West, we've had a break, could be very important, sir. The police at Basingstoke have just found Miss Prell's suit jacket. Buried in some rubble near the site of the new by-pass, sir — it was turned up by a bull-dozer which is levelling the earth there. They say there's no doubt it's the same coat, there's actually a name tag with the Salisbury firm of Murrow & Son where she bought it. How about *that*?"

Roger felt a stab of excitement and at the same time, one of dread. Thoughts tumbled through his mind. Why only the coat? If they'd killed her, why take the coat off? Could it be a deliberate false lead?

"I think we ought to get after that as fast as we can," he said. "I'll ask Mr. Kempton to go to Basingstoke at once."

"I told the local police I was sure you would be along soon," Venables said, a little more subdued. "One other thing, sir. Caldicott was still at Lords half-an-hour ago, and no one's been in touch with him so far."

"Thanks," Roger said. "Bye." He rang off and went on to Kempton without any change of tone: "They've found the linen jacket of the girl's suit near Basingstoke. I'll call Basingstoke H.Q. and have someone meet you on the road — just this side of the by-pass or a little nearer here. I'll make sure they do any bull-dozing carefully — but they will in any case. If you're asked, say I'll be over as soon as I've cleared up some work here."

"Right, sir," Kempton said. "I'll be on my way."

He went out like a shot, and Roger smiled faintly, thinking: he may be a dull stick but he doesn't waste a second. He lifted the receiver, started to say: "Give me —" and then changed his mind. "Never mind, I'll go and see him." He followed Kempton out and reached Isherwood's door, which was ajar. He tapped and went in and Isherwood looked up from something he was writing.

"Jack," Roger said. "Linda Prell's jacket's been found near Basingstoke. I've sent Kempton out and I need a word with someone there who can get things moving."

"Bull," said Isherwood promptly.

"What —"

"Sorry — Chief Inspector Bull," Isherwood explained, and stretched out for the telephone. "I'll get him for you." He said into the mouthpiece: "Mr. Bull, Basingstoke," and put the receiver down but didn't speak for a moment. Then heavily he wondered aloud: "Do you think this means they'll find the body? Are you —" The telephone bell rang and he snatched up the receiver. "Monty? . . . Jack . . . Handsome West is here and he'd like a word with you. Guess what about?"

Bull, Roger was thinking. I knew a Bull at Hendon.

"Hallo, Chief Inspector, I'm told you've made a find out there."

A man with a rather high-pitched voice answered: "A bull-dozer operator has. What would you like us to do?"

"Dig," Roger said. "Preferably not with the bull-dozer."

"I get your point. We've already cordoned off the area and started checking. I can tell you one thing, Mr. West. A car with new Dunlop tyres was on that spot either yesterday or late the day before. There are clear tyre prints in the chalk —"

"Chalk?"

"The subsoil out there is all chalk and a lot was turned up when they made the motorway." If Bull's voice were a little higher it would be falsetto. "And that stuff's hard to get out of tyre treads and from underneath any car."

"Ah!" breathed Roger. "Thanks. I'm tied up here for a while but Kempton's coming over. He started out five minutes ago. Can you have someone on the outskirts to meet him?"

"Yes," Bull answered. "But I hope you'll be able to come, too."

"Oh, yes — the moment I can," Roger assured him. "Thanks."

He rang off, and rested his hand on the telephone. Isherwood, also in quiet mood, lit a cigarette and sat back in his chair. Roger told him of Kempton's news, the Bodenham number, and his visit to Withers, all in a curiously flat voice. He really wanted to be on the way to Basingstoke, at the scene of action, but first he wanted to check on Withers. Isherwood simply said: "Not Withers, I don't believe it," and looked shocked. Then he added: "Didn't you say Batten's often been out to one of the flats there, with Linda Prell?"

"Yes," answered Roger; and he wondered where Batten was now.

And he wondered about the white patch, very like chalk, which had been on the drive outside Withers's house.

*   *   *

Batten was in the little flat where he had spent so many gloriously happy hours with Linda. Her sister and brother-in-law were both out, and he was sitting back in an easy chair, physically comfortable, emotionally near the end of his tether. In a strange way, both West and Isherwood had added to the distress; he had never dreamed that Isherwood would show any sympathy or understanding.

He was half-drowsing, for he had not slept well for several nights, when the telephone bell rang. It was on the other side of this pleasant room which overlooked a courtyard with a black-painted lamp in the middle. Should he answer? There was really no reason why he shouldn't let it go unanswered, it would almost certainly be for the others and the caller might wonder why he was there.

Brrr-brrr. Brrr-brrr. Brrr-brrr. It went on and on.

He didn't have to say who he was!

He got up and crossed to the door and a small table on which the instrument stood. He picked it up and spoke in a slurred voice:

"This is Bodenham 665."

"And that is Detective Sergeant Batten," a man said. He did not go on; just left the words hanging with a hint of menace. "And that is Detective Sergeant Batten." Who was the caller? Batten wondered with a sudden revival of acute fear. A newspaperman — oh God, no! He gulped before he said:

"Who — who is that?"

"That's one of the things you'll never be able to find out," the man replied. His voice had a slight London or Cockney twang. "Do you want to see her alive again?"

Batten cried: "See *Linda*?"

"Or Woman Detective Constable Prell, the naughty, naughty little gel."

"Oh God," Batten groaned. "Don't joke. Don't torment me. Is she — is she alive?"

"She is alive but not so well is Detective Constable Linda Prell."

"Please," Batten begged. Sweat was pouring down his face. "Please tell me — is she all right?"

"She isn't the happiest woman in the world but in the circumstances she's a very lucky one," the man said.

"Where — where is she?"

"Safely hidden from digging eyes."

"Digging!"

"You have very good hearing." There was a pause before the man went on in a much sharper tone: "Listen to me, Batten. We buried her jacket out at Basingstoke to draw off the top cops so that we could have a quiet word with you. Don't get anything wrong. She's alive now, but I personally will cut her throat if you don't do exactly what I tell you. Understand?"

"What — what — what do you want?"

"First things first. Don't tell anyone I called you," the man said. "Just get it into your pig-head that if you talk to any-one, West or Isherwood or Linda Prell's sister or brother-in-law, she won't live for five minutes. There's only one way to save her life: by doing exactly what I tell you. It's a special job and I'll tell you about it later."

The speaker put down the telephone noisily, and it seemed a long time before silence settled in Batten's ears. He stood looking at the wall. Linda's sister, Meg, had put a small framed picture there, one of an Italian coast village set in a charming little fretwork frame. In it he saw the reflection of the lamp in the courtyard as it switched on. His fingers shook as he replaced the receiver. Slowly, slowly, he turned round and went back to the armchair.

How did they know he was here?

They must have been checking on him for days; probably weeks.

He moved before sitting down and went to the window. It was still broad daylight, although the light had gone: the lamp had a time switch which didn't keep time with the light evenings. He saw a car turn into the drive — a Rover — West had a Rover. The car disappeared behind some bushes and reappeared, going very slowly.

It was West.

What the devil was the Yard man doing here? Had he come to see him, Batten? He was in no shape to see anyone, he simply couldn't talk to West in this mood. He would see how badly shaken he was, would be on to him with unrelenting questions.

The car passed, going towards the main house. That didn't

mean he was safe, West might be looking for him and have lost his way. What other reason could there possibly be? He couldn't see the main house from here and it was five minutes before he felt fairly sure West hadn't come to see him. Thank God! He looked across the courtyard and over the trees towards green and distant hills. There was a stillness everywhere; and the light had taken on a strange clarity. The furthest hill, two miles away from here, was known as Hazebury Ring, from where there was a magnificent view by day.

The telephone bell shrilled out. He jumped wildly and his heart thumped. He turned to look at the instrument. *Brrr-brrr. Brrr-brrr. Brrr-brrr.* It couldn't be the man again, could it? Not so soon. He wouldn't answer. *Brrr-brrr. Brrr-brrr.* The ringing sound was like a magnet, drawing him. He moved towards the instrument, and at last lifted the receiver.

"Who — who is that?" he asked huskily.

"I told you before, that's one of the things you'll never find out," the man said, as if he had not been off the line. "*Do* you want her alive?"

"I'll do anything to save her!"

"Anything?"

"Yes, I swear it!" gasped Batten. "What do you want me to do?"

"I'll tell you when I'm ready," the man said. "Be at Hazebury Ring at midnight. Don't be even a minute late."

"Don't ring off!" cried Batten. "Don't ring off!"

There was a funny little sound at the other end of the line, as if the receiver had already gone down, but the Cockney voice sounded again, sharply.

"What's that?"

"Don't go."

"You be at Hazebury Ring tonight if you want to sleep with your precious mistress again," the man said harshly. "Don't make any mistake."

"How do I know she's alive?" Batten gasped. "Tell me that."

"You just have to take my word for it."

"Well, I won't! Before I'll do anything I must have proof she's alive."

Without a word, the other man rang off. Batten did exactly

as he had before, going slowly to the window. It was still daylight but something of the pristine brightness had gone. He was quivering and felt sticky-hot. One of the other tenants walked across the courtyard, and disappeared through an arched gateway. He felt as if he were stuck to the floor and simply could not move. Yet his mind worked. If the telephone caller knew Hazebury Ring it was near-conclusive proof that he had studied the district well, or else had been primed by someone who lived locally.

Who?

The telephone bell rang: *Brrrrrr!*

He snatched up the receiver and barked: "Who is that?"

"Tom," Linda said in a broken voice. "Tom, don't let them make you do anything. Don't let the Force down. Tom, I —" There was a moment of silence and then as if from a long way off the man said: "Hazebury Ring twelve midnight," and the line went dead.

*   *   *

The dark slope of Hazebury Ring, like the breast of a reclining woman, was just visible from the window; above it were the stars, growing brighter as the daylight faded into afterglow.

*   *   *

Thirty miles in the other direction, on the chalk downs just outside Basingstoke, men were digging under floodlights, and every clod and lump of chalk, every stone and every piece of rubble was examined closely, for human blood or flesh, for hair, and for a woman's clothes which were not there.

*   *   *

Close by, on Tom Batten's doorstep, Roger West was talking again to the owner of Newall Lodge and Stable House, silver-haired John Withers.

15

John Withers

THE ROOM on the ground floor was lined with books. One wall was covered with leather-bound volumes, and there were more on either side of the huge fireplace. A crescent of chairs surrounded the fireplace, in front of a huge, empty grate where brightly polished brass dogs glowed. The curtains had not yet been drawn but lights shone from big lamp standards over each man's head. Withers was remarkable for that very good complexion and clear eyes; he was quiet-voiced and pleasant, might even be called urbane. Outside in a galleried hall Roger had seen paintings which might be very old and of great value. There was an atmosphere of wealth and luxury everywhere.

Withers was saying: "I'm glad you were able to come back, Mr. West. I've had time to recall all the details — things easily get blurred, you know. I first had a call from this man Stephenson on the afternoon before the private view at Leech's place. He said he had heard of my collection through a mutual friend and asked if he could see it. I'm as fond of showing the paintings as I am the trees, so cheerfully said yes. He brought his wife." Withers smiled most disarmingly. "Stephenson wanted to buy some of my pictures — I have quite a collection of the new fashion, Victoriana. But I don't buy and sell paintings for money, I buy when I like and sell when I'm tired of some I have. Likes and dislikes are much the same as fashions, you know. They change." He smiled and raised his hands. "Perhaps they make fashions!"

"How long have you known Mr. Stephenson?" Roger asked.

"Oh, I hardly know him at all."

"How did you come to meet him?"

"The mutual friend is a man I've known on and off for several years," answered Withers. "A Frank Caldicott, one of the best judges of paintings I've ever known. After Stephenson went back to Salisbury, we met again in the bar of the Rose and Briar. The Stephensons were staying there, and there were only two or three at the bar. Tom Batten was one — but perhaps I should be more formal and call him Detective Sergeant Batten!" The eyes behind the tinted glasses smiled.

"Tom will do," Roger said. "I understand that Linda Prell is often in one of your flats."

"She stays with her sister who lives at Stable House," Withers agreed, "but it won't help to ask me about that, Mr. West. I don't know what the tenants do and within limits I don't care. Provided they pay their rent and behave like pleasant human beings I don't bother them and I don't know much about their coming and going." He picked up his glass. "Sure you won't have another drink?"

"Quite sure, thanks," Roger said. "And I must go." But he made no move to get up. "How often has Mr. Stephenson telephoned you?"

"Oh — two or three times from Bristol and once from Bath."

The answer came pat but did not explain the furtive way in which, according to the Bristol police, Stephenson had obtained this number.

"Always after your pictures?"

"He is a very persistent man."

"How well do you know Caldicott?"

"Only casually as an individual," answered Withers. "We used to play cricket for a London club side and had a couple of seasons together. That must be twenty years ago, I haven't played for ten years. He was in his teens then and I was already nearly past the playing days. He came to see me once to ask if he could look out for pictures for me but I like to collect my own. I get twice as much fun out of discovering a picture in a junk shop as I do buying one from a gallery like Leech's. I'm not a very good customer for the regular dealers, I'm afraid. I do wish you would have that other drink."

"I really mustn't, I've a long drive to do," Roger said, and at last he got up. "How well do you know Tom Batten, sir?"

"About as well as everyone in Salisbury does. He's a joiner. A member of this club and that, one of the guardians of the cathedral — one of the best guides to the cathedral and the close, for that matter. He's always prepared to help with any charity or good cause, but as a man I don't really know him at all." Withers also stood up, smiled a little deprecatingly, and went on: "How many people do you really know as men?"

Roger laughed.

"Touché," he said. "And thanks again for your help."

"I'm afraid I've been no help at all," deplored Withers, opening the door on to the galleried hall. It seemed much brighter than Roger had noticed before and several of the large pictures were individually lit. "I wish you had time to look at my little collection. Hardly a square inch of the wall uncovered, you see." He moved back so that Roger could see up to the gallery, and it was true; every part of the wall about the staircase and above the gallery was covered with paintings. After a moment he led the way to the front door. "Goodnight, Mr. West."

They shook hands on Roger's 'Goodnight'.

Roger got in the car as Withers went back indoors, leaving the porch light on; it glowed on a white patch and two or three small lumps of a white substance. He got out of the car and bent close to a front wheel, as if checking the tyre, but he picked up two of the little lumps and slipped them into his pocket.

Soon, he drove slowly down the drive, the tyres crunching on gravel. A light from another lamp at the foot of the drive shone on some white stones. Lights showed at several windows in the Old Stables and in the village. It was peaceful and even idyllic, until a man sprang out of the hedge on one side, only a few feet from the road. Roger jammed on his brakes, and had time to wind down his window as a man said:

"Sorry."

From just behind him there came a click and a flash.

"I didn't mean to scare the wits out of you," the nearer man said. "I'm Childs of the *Herald*. You haven't a nice new angle for me, have you?"

Roger hesitated. His heart was still palpitating and fright had brought a flush of annoyance, but exasperation would get him nowhere and he wondered if he could use this man to help. So he asked:

"Have you heard about the jacket found at Basingstoke?"

"Yes, but my orders are to stay near the heart of this crime, which is wherever you are." In the lamplight and the faint afterglow, Childs's face showed round and pleasant; his photographer was a long-haired boy. "Do you think that was a false scent?"

"No," Roger said. "I don't think one way or the other."

"Think she's dead?" asked Childs, abruptly.

"I've no evidence whether she's dead or alive," Roger answered. "Are you really here to talk to me or did you come to worry the life out of Linda Prell's relatives?"

"They're out for the evening," Childs said. "I'm told to stick to you like glue but I checked the Prell relatives when you were in with John Withers, and got no answer. What do you think about the rumours of a mystery lover, Mr. West?"

"If it's true, Linda Prell's as human as the next attractive woman."

"And if it's not true, she isn't!"

"If it's not true, it indicates what I've already been told."

"What?"

"She's a dedicated policewoman."

"Well, well!" exclaimed Childs. "So I have a new angle after all. Do you know what she was after?"

"You mean, what she may have discovered?"

"Yes."

"No."

"Any idea what the whole schemozzle is about?" asked Childs lightly. "Is it some big plot such as the Great Train Robbery? The Great Art Theft, for instance. Stephenson and Caldicott and Withers here are all involved and the *Herald*'s New York spies tell us that the New York police have been consulted by you chaps. I couldn't use the angle of a great international Art Theft Conspiracy, could I?"

"I'm not your editor," Roger retorted.

"*Have* you checked with New York?"

"Yes."

"About Stephenson?"

"You know perfectly well that I can't answer such a question."

"Ah!"

"But I do think that the missing police officer possibly stumbled on a plot of considerable magnitude," Roger told him, and added in a tone of finality: "Let's call it a day. I have to drive out to Basingstoke, I gather I'll see you there."

"No dinner, now no supper," groaned Childs. But he smiled. "What's this about some new and highly significant appointment for you at the Yard, Mr. West?"

He made the mistake of speaking slowly and smiling as if about to spring a surprise, and the word 'appointment' warned Roger what was coming. So he was able to look blank, and then to ask:

"What's that?" Then he rubbed his chin. "It's news to me."

"Well, I hope it's good news," Childs said, cheerfully. "Are you really going to Basingstoke now?"

"Yes."

"Couldn't possibly wait for half-an-hour while we get a snack, could you?"

"I'm going to get one at my pub," Roger said. "I'm told they have good snacks at the bar there." He nodded, and started the engine again and made off, as the two newspaper-men disappeared.

The next time he saw them was at the site of the digging.

He went to the hotel and telephoned Isherwood, then ordered some sandwiches and coffee in his room. When Isherwood arrived, the two pieces of white substance were on a piece of brown paper, hard and damp in the middle and powdery outside.

"And you found those outside Withers's front door?" Isherwood said gloomily.

"Yes. It's chalk — and we shouldn't have much trouble checking where it came from," said Roger.

Isherwood simply nodded.

*   *   *

Two small mechanical diggers were being worked to loosen up the chalk where it had gone solid. At least a dozen building workers and as many policemen plied spades. These went 'sough' into the damp clay-like chalk, 'sough' as they came out. Over in one spot, near the floodlights which had been rigged up much as at Gorley Wood, a team of six men were using sieves for the drier soil, and breaking up other lumps with chisels and hammers. So far there was only a pile of beer and soft drink cans, bottles and bottle tops, cigarette packets, matches, a few odds and ends, some obviously used sheaths. Kempton, with a tall thin man, were close by the mechanical digger. Roger joined them.

"Why, hallo, sir!" Kempton sprang almost to attention. "You haven't met Chief Inspector Bull, have you?"

"No. Hallo, Chief Inspector."

"Superintendent."

They shook hands, then Roger was taken over the site. It was beneath the actual motorway and had been one of the main construction areas. Trees on one side had not been disturbed but on the site itself had been mercilessly cut down. Some parts were dry; some seemed to suck at Roger's shoes. He was impressed by the speed and thoroughness with which the digging had been arranged, but troubled because it might go on for days and remain inconclusive.

He took out the chalk he had found, and there seemed little doubt it had come from here. It would have to be analysed, of course, it wasn't yet evidence; but it seemed very significant, and for the first time he felt fiercely hopeful about the case.

Suddenly, one of the men on the mechanical diggers called: "Over here! Over here!" There was such excitement in his voice that everyone looked round while Roger and his party started towards the spot. They couldn't hurry because of the soggy chalk patches. One spot was cordoned off and two men were examining tyre prints; there were two new-looking tyres close by. Roger was a pace behind Kempton and a pace ahead of Bull getting to the mechanical digger.

There was just one fear in Roger's mind: that the body had been found.

It wasn't a body, it was a single shoe, a new-looking shoe despite the chalk clinging to it. And five minutes later enough chalk had been cleaned off to show that it was of the same pattern-flowered linen as the suit.

"That means we'll have to go through the night, presumably," Bull said.

"I really think we should," Roger agreed.

"It'll cost a fortune in overtime," Bull grumbled. "But I'll give the orders. I *had* hoped to stop at midnight."

* * *

Above the stables at Bodenham there was a clock which struck the hours and sent the notes quivering about the grounds and nearby village. Sometimes, thrown by a trick of the wind or a shallow valley in the ground, it carried for miles, and it carried to the foot of Hazebury Ring as Tom Batten stood waiting for someone to materialise. He had been here for fifteen minutes, anxious not to be late. The stars were very bright and there was a slim crescent of moon, showing the trees which surrounded what had been a Roman mound. The lights of the city spread wide, the street lamps mostly yellow, and here and there yellow spots of light showed at windows. Villages showed in little clusters, and above all this glowed the red light on top of the cathedral spire.

It was eerie in the near-darkness.

Hardly a leaf or a branch stirred, the night was so still. The rustling of small animals was just audible; now and again an owl flew, silent but for wings beating the air. Batten could hear his own breathing and the beating of his heart.

Out of the shadows and the silence a man called: "Batten."

Batten's heart leapt wildly.

"Who — who — who is there?"

"Batten," the caller said, "come down about twenty yards. Straight down."

Twenty yards, repeated Batten to himself. Say about thirty paces. The going was fairly even and he stumbled only once against a molehill or a rabbit mound. He could see and hear nothing.

"That's far enough." The man was now close to his side. Batten stopped.

"Don't move and don't try to find out where I am," the man said. "And don't forget: she's alive. She'll stay alive if you do exactly what you're told. If you don't, she will die and so will you."

Batten managed to mutter: "What do you want?"

"You're one of the special guardians of the cathedral, aren't you?"

"The cathedral!"

"That's what I said. Are you a cathedral guardian, or aren't you?"

"Yes," muttered Batten. "Yes, I am."

"Can you get in the cathedral any time you want to?"

"Yes, but —"

"Never mind the buts. Do you have a pass key?"

"Yes, but —"

Just behind Batten there was a rustle of movement, and he gasped and half-turned. He caught a glimpse of a man, saw him clearly enough to see that the face was masked, saw a hand upraised and felt a searing slash across his shoulders, nigh unbearable pain which made him cry out. And he staggered but kept his footing. Blood was racing through his ears, and he began to gasp for breath. Then, he felt cord at his wrists, felt it loop, felt them pulled and tied together behind him. Over the noises which he made himself, the speaker said:

"I told you no buts. You do as you're told, or that whore Prell will feel a lot more than that whip before she dies."

Batten gritted his teeth, to keep back the words which wanted to spill out, words of hatred, rage, vengeance. His whole body was aquiver with these emotions and with fear. He waited, half-expecting another blow. Instead, the man — who was Ledbetter — went on:

"Do you have a pass key to the cathedral?"

"Yes."

"Where is it?"

"On — on my chain."

"Do you have a key to the library?"

"Yes," Batten muttered. "But —" He broke off, knowing it would be useless to argue. "Yes. But the library's protected by — by an electronic contact system. If you opened the door or even tried to, you'd have the Chief Security Officer out in ten seconds and the police in two minutes."

After a long silence, Ledbetter said: "*You* can break the contact, can't you?"

"Like hell I would!" gasped Batten.

"If you don't, Linda Prell will die," said Ledbetter. "And all the world will know she was a whore and you one of her lovers." He waited for a few seconds, and then went on: "Can you break the contact?"

"Yes," muttered Batten. "Yes, I can."

"That's better," Ledbetter said. "You've got some sense after all. Keep on being sensible and you'll have fun with Linda again. So you can break the electronic contact with the alarm system and you have a key to the library. Where is it?"

"On my chain," Batten muttered. "I told you."

"What do you carry a key for?"

"There — there's always a danger of fire."

"Fire," the man echoed. "There's other danger to that whore —"

"Don't keep calling her a whore!" cried Batten.

"What would you rather me call her? Your tart? If you don't do exactly what I tell you, she'll die. I'll take a lot of pleasure in raping her first."

Batten drew in a searing breath.

"How often do you go to the cathedral at night when you're on duty?" demanded the speaker in the shadows.

"Two — two or three times."

"Any set time?"

"No."

"You and how many others?"

"Only — only the Chief Security Officer and a few policemen."

"Do you work on a rota system or a shift system?"

"Ro-rota," answered Batten. Speaking hurt his voice and thinking was sheer horror. "We — we take a night each, it only takes half-an-hour or so to walk through and check everything. It's — it's mostly a fire precaution. We — we fit in with our jobs. We —"

"Are you all cops?"

"No," said Batten. "No! Two of us are in the Force, there's a garage security man, two night watchmen, two nurses — anyone who has night shifts and can get half-an-hour off, can join in. All they do is go and make sure everything's all right, it doesn't take long I tell you. If there looks like any trouble, they call police headquarters."

"That's good," said the man in the shadows thinly. "That's *very* good. Who's on duty tonight?"

"I don't know!" gasped Batten. "I really don't know. Someone will go and have a look at the place. They'll look inside the cathedral and go up to the library where the copy of Magna Carta is. They —"

He broke off, and actually cringed back, although there was no immediate threat from behind him, no horror but his own realisation. When he spoke again his voice was little more than a croak.

"No! *No!* Not that —"

"Don't you make any mistake, just that," the man said. "And you're going to get it for us."

Batten stood still; and silent. His heart had stopped thumping and he hardly seemed to be breathing. An owl hooted; there was a cackle of birds, disturbed by fox or cat; then silence again. He did not speak but words seemed to echo inside his head.

I would rather die than that, he thought.

And then he thought: but would Linda rather die?

He asked in a croaking voice: "How do I know she's alive?"

16

Alive . . .

THE QUESTION took the unseen man by surprise. He drew in his breath, audibly. Rustling behind Batten warned him that the other man had moved and might strike again. He braced himself but no blow came. Only a rasped:

"You heard her!"

"How could I be sure it was Linda?"

"You'd know her voice, wouldn't you?"

"I wasn't *sure*."

The man didn't answer.

Batten wondered what hope there was left; whether he could defy them even without his fears for Linda. Contrarily he wondered whether, even for Linda, he could do what this man wanted. He warned himself that these men could knock him over the head now and take his keys. He couldn't prevent this. It would be easier for them if he did the work but he couldn't prevent them from doing what they wanted once they had the keys.

The keys felt heavy against his thigh; he kept them on a ring inside his trouser waistband.

He thought, agonised: what would Linda —

And then he knew that whatever Linda would do, whether it meant the difference between life and death for her or for him, he could not help them; he had to stop them.

Minutes were ticking by. He wasn't sure why there had not been a word after he had said: "I wasn't sure." It was almost as if something had frightened them away. Nonsense! He would have heard them moving.

The man in the shadows said: "If I let you see her, will you do it?"

That was how much he wanted to be guided into the cathedral. Oh God! What would make men plan such a thing as this? The Sarum Magna Carta. The best of those surviving. A piece of England. A piece of history. The foundation of the rights of Englishmen.

He couldn't do it.

Nothing would ever make him do it.

Not even sight of Linda alive.

Could they let him see her? Here on this dark hillside? It made no sense, nothing made any sense to him.

As that thought came the movement was repeated behind him and a man gripped his bound arms and thrust him forward. He heard the first man moving through the undergrowth and suddenly saw a light, a pale light as from a lamp. The nearer he got the brighter the light seemed. It was in one of the little, shallow caves that abounded in Hazebury Ring and in all the countryside about here. Children often came and played by day; the more daring came by night. He was pushed close; a hand at his neck thrust his head down and the second man said in a high-pitched voice:

"Get in!"

He stumbled to his knees and then edged himself forward over dirt and stones until he saw her, stretched out at the back of the cave.

He *saw* her.

She *was* alive.

She wore only her slip and stockings, nothing else; just slip and stockings. Her face was turned towards him. She was gagged so that she couldn't speak, but her eyes spoke for her. She was in terror. *Terror*. She lay on uneven ground of the cave and the light fell on her forehead and her great eyes which pleaded for her.

The man spoke from behind Batten.

"You do what I tell you or we'll just have a little fun and then kill her. All we have to do is fill that hole in. No one will ever find her in a thousand years."

Please, please, please, her eyes seemed to say.

And he loved her.

She had often waited for him like this, touched with a kind of shyness which vanished the moment he was beside her. *Linda.* There she was, and she was terrified. He did not doubt that the man would carry out his threat. One thing was certain: he had to promise to do what they wanted; he had to leave her here at least with hope.

He said: "I'll — I'll do it."

The words seemed to echo: *I'll do-do-do it.*

And her eyes seemed to blaze: *Thank you my love, thank you my darling.*

Then the men behind pulled him away.

*   *   *

Linda Prell lay, watching him.

From the moment she had been kidnapped she had alternated between quivering fear and stoic resignation. She had been in a stupor of drugged sleep most of the time, but occasionally she had woken, to solitude; had been visited by the youth, and then given a little food, soup and biscuits and water, allowed to relieve herself and then tied up and drugged again.

She knew that one of the places where she had come round had been a small caravan, pulled by a car which made little noise.

There had been an old shed, stinking of rotten meat and paint.

And there had been this cave.

They had brought her up here after dark, not talking to her but talking to each other. Only now and again did she catch a full sentence but gradually a picture formed in her mind. They wanted Tom to help them steal something from the cathedral. *Something.* What sacred relic could they want? What could be of such value as to make all this worthwhile?

Then the older man had said: "That bloody charter," and she knew.

At first, she had been shocked beyond feeling. Until then she had hated the thought of Tom conniving at a theft under any kind of pressure, for she knew that it would sear him for the rest of his days. But *the* great treasure: Magna Carta!

As a girl at one of the schools nearby she had been brought to see it; at the school she had been taught to reverence it because of its significance as well as its age. To her it was less Magna Carta, the *démarche* of the barons but more like a bone of the hand of Christ or part of the wood from the cross he had carried. It was not part of ordinary life: it was sacred.

Nothing must make him agree to do this thing: nothing!

And there he was, with that face she had come to like and love, the little piggy of a face, saying in a voice she could hardly hear, it was so hoarse: "I'll do it."

"No!" she wanted to scream. "No, no, no! Let them kill me, let them do anything with me but don't help them. Don't help them!" She tried to make him understand by the way she looked at him. "No, no, no!"

Yet it seemed to him that she was saying: "Thank you my love, thank you my darling."

*   *   *

Roger watched the mechanical digger turn up another yard of chalky earth; watched men going through the fresh pile with forks and trowels; saw the crowd which was getting bigger and bigger. Every now and again something was found; once, a diamond ring worth several hundred pounds. A pair of dentures wired together; several keys, old silver, cups — anything which might be picked up by the dustmen. Calls came over the walkie-talkie, none of them important. It was approaching midnight and getting chilly, and the crowd was beginning to disperse when a call came for Roger. As he went towards the car a woman from a canteen called:

"Like tea or coffee, sir?"

"Tea, please." Roger took a proffered cup.

"Can you spare a poor newspaperman a cup of coffee, too?" Childs asked.

"Poor newspaperman be blowed," the woman retorted. "I'd wrap all you chaps round fish and chips if I had my way. Sugar?"

"Please," Childs said humbly, and his photographer, taking a cup, said: "No sugar, ta."

Roger reached the car on which the message was being

relayed, got inside, balanced the tea on top of the dashboard, and said:

"West speaking."

"Hullo, Mr. West." It was Isherwood in his most formal voice, which suggested that he had someone with him. "I thought you ought to hear of this right away. Tom Batten is missing."

Roger actually gasped: *"What?"*

"I'm afraid it's true," said Isherwood. "His wife telephoned us five minutes ago. He said he was going home early but he hasn't been there. We tried his — I mean Linda Prell's sister — and she said he'd been in; he has a key. But he'd gone before eleven o'clock, when they got back. They'd been out to the girl's parents to try to reassure them. He'd made himself some coffee, and hadn't been gone for long because the saucepan he'd boiled some milk in was still warm."

"Anything else?" demanded Roger.

"Not yet," said Isherwood. "But I've got half-a-dozen men out in the Bodenham area, they're going to knock on doors to find out if he's been seen. He might have other friends there. And the pubs were closing when he left, someone in any of the nearby villages might have seen him."

"Can you put every available man on this?" asked Roger.

"Half a mo'," Isherwood said, and his voice sounded fainter: he was talking either to someone else in the office or on another telephone. He was soon back talking to Roger. "Yes, I'll send round for all who are off duty. You'd recommend checking all the local villages, wouldn't you?"

Roger said: "Jack, what about that thing we were talking about?"

"I haven't forgotten it," Isherwood said. "Why?"

"The cathedral ought to be very carefully watched," Roger said.

"I hadn't reckoned on there being an attempt so soon." Isherwood's tone was almost one of complaint. "But — oh, you're right, of course. Would you station the men close or —" He broke off, saying: "Just a moment, please." His north-country accent was very noticeable tonight, as if he usually made an effort to control it. There was a mumble of voices before his came loud again: "You'd have them kept at a distance, wouldn't you?"

"At places from which they can move quickly if they see anything suspicious," Roger answered. "A few men near Newall Lodge might be a good idea, too."

"I can't *make* men!" Isherwood exploded.

"Is the Western Federation Chief Constable with you?"

"Yes," answered Isherwood.

"Then ask him if he'll borrow some men from Hampshire, Southampton and Bournemouth if needs be," Roger said crisply.

"I will put it to him," Isherwood promised. "How long will you be, sir?"

"Less than an hour," answered Roger. "Will you keep me posted as I come?"

"Yes, of course." Isherwood rang off, and Roger put the receiver down slowly and picked up his tea. It was nearly cold. He got out as Bull came up, with Childs and his photographer as close as a shadow. "There's a new development at Salisbury," he said. "I'm going straight back. May I take Kempton?"

"Of course," Bull said. "Significant?"

Childs was not now the only newspaperman in sight; others had crowded round and four cameras were poised. Yet Bull should be told, and there seemed no reason for secrecy, so Roger stated clearly:

"Tom Batten is missing."

"Batten," Childs echoed, and the name seemed to move from lip to lip as the newspapermen crowded round. "Batten — Batten — Batten. How? When? How long ago? When was he last seen? Is he being searched for? How do you know? where?" The questions flooded in, all to the point, even if some were repetitive. "Anything found here? The girl, I mean? Arms? Legs? Trinkets?"

At last, Roger was pointing the car towards the open road, with several Press cars strung out behind him and Kempton sitting stolidly by his side, as if telling himself that Roger must have had all the questions he could take for a long time, and he, Kempton, would be the soul of patience.

Roger put his foot down hard and the needle hovered between eighty and ninety.

"Batten's in a bad way," he said at last.

"Afraid he might kill himself?" asked Kempton.

"It's not inconceivable, but —" Roger broke off, and asked: "Any idea what all this is about, Alan?"

"I wouldn't go as far as that," Kempton answered.

"How far would you go?" demanded Roger.

"Well," said Kempton, "if I started with Salisbury and some funny business in fine art, heard that a top American contact man for secret buyers was involved, discovered that whoever was behind it was offering big money, and using someone prepared to abduct a police officer — well, I'd add all that up to something very big. Such as —" He paused and now the tone in his voice was defiant but dogged: "I'd guess Magna Carta." Then in a sighing voice, he added: "It can't be, can it?"

"It might be," Roger said. "You've added most of the things up in the same way that I would."

"But who the devil would — oh, well, if you think it's on the cards it probably is," Kempton said. "I've shied away from the idea." He was thoughtful for some seconds, and then asked: "Any idea who it is?"

"Only guesses," Roger told him. "Now I'm going to concentrate on driving."

*   *   *

Police were sent over the county borders and from the two County Borough forces, and slowly and carefully a cordon was placed around Salisbury cathedral. Another, smaller one, cordoned off Bodenham village. Roger was told of progress as he drove, the loudspeaker distorted in the onrushing car.

"North and east cathedral now covered both inside and outside the walls."

"South side covered from inside only."

"Main gate and two supplementary gates already locked. Now under close surveillance."

"No sign of intruders."

"South side now covered from outside and west wall both inside and outside."

"Roofs of buildings in the close now being used for surveillance."

"Bodenham village now completely closed off."

These messages came one upon the other, but there was no report of anyone inside or outside even when Roger reached the city limits, a little before one-fifteen. Now three possibilities haunted him. First, that he was wrong and no raid was planned. Second, that the raid had already taken place. Third, that the raiders might already be in the cathedral and hampered in their getaway.

What would happen if they were?

Would they damage Magna Carta out of malice? Would they even threaten to damage or destroy if they were not allowed to go free?

He was going through an agonising appraisal of the facts when a call came through from Bath to say that Stephenson had left, by himself, and was driving towards Salisbury.

"Let him come," Roger decided, and hoped it wasn't a wrong decision. Was Stephenson planning to be in at the kill, after all? And *were* the other three inside the cathedral or not?

*　　　*　　　*

They were already in the library — Tom Batten and Ledbetter and Ledbetter's young mate, the specialist in electronics, whose name was Bryce.

They had not yet found how to get the copy of Magna Carta away.

They did not know that they were surrounded.

17

The Theft

To BATTEN, normally, it was the most beautiful sight in the world.

The stars were very bright and the light from the lamps in the city and in the close and at the house surrounding it shone upon the huge grey edifice and seemed to make it translucent; as if the grey of centuries had been lifted off and the original white stone, cut out of quarries only twelve miles away, restored on every wall. It was as if the night breathed life into the stone.

The outline of houses, some as old, some older than the cathedral, made an uneven line against the sky. The trees, some old and tall, some little more than saplings, were still like the trees at Hazebury Ring. One huge cedar stood like a clutch of dragons, each pointed limb a fang.

Batten had come here as a choir boy; he had come here as a worshipper; he had been a member of the guardians of the cathedral since he had joined the police force. This was part of him as it was part of England.

It was so still and quiet. Sounds from beyond ·the walls were muted, except for the rustling made by the men there was no sound at all.

It was as if the cathedral and the close around it and all the people who lived nearby, were sleeping.

Now, Ledbetter was on one side of him and Bryce on the other, making faint sounds as they walked from St. Anne's Gate, which was always the last to be locked.

No one else moved; not even lovers, who had long since left the sanctuary of walls and shadows.

Ledbetter's car was parked on the main road near the gate, where it was legal to park even at night. They had left Linda alone in her dread, and a picture of her face seemed to show on the spire. Batten could almost hear her breathing, see the pleading in her eyes.

Ledbetter whispered: "You know what to do?"

"Yes."

"Don't make any mistake," Ledbetter warned.

Batten didn't answer.

"He'd better not," Bryce said. "Or that bitch will be broken into pieces."

"For God's sake —" Batten began.

"Shut up!"

They reached the porch of the north entrance and stood still looking at the walls which surrounded the lawns, but saw only empty parked cars. No heads, no faces.

"No one's watching," Ledbetter said. "We've fooled them."

'They'd better not watch," Bryce said in his newer, savage voice. "Batten — do you know what will happen if West or anyone else tries to stop us?"

"I know."

"I've ten little fire bombs and they can all be triggered off by the detonator switch in my hands. Electronics, see. I left one back with the woman." He slid his hand into Batten's pocket and went on: "Now you've got one close to your belly. Open the door."

Batten could remember the youth fiddling with electric batteries, but had no idea what he had been doing; it must have been this. If it were true, if he could start fire by remote control, how could he be stopped?

It was very dark inside the porch. Batten normally had a torch, but now had to grope for the keyhole; at last he found it. The door creaked. Ledbetter, carrying a lightweight fire-proof container in which to place the document, banged against the stone walls; the metal clanged.

"Quiet!" breathed Bryce.

Even Ledbetter muttered: "Sorry."

They crept inside, and stood in the silent stillness; and the chill which struck from walls and pillars, floor and stained glass seemed to penetrate their bodies. Gradually the windows began to glow with eerie light; and Ledbetter shone a torch. The beam of a torch crept round. Nothing moved and Ledbetter whispered: "Which way?"

"We go straight towards the nave," Batten said.

"Where's that old clock?" demanded Bryce. "The oldest in the world, don't they call it?"

"Yes, it — it's up there." Batten pointed to the right.

"Wait here," Bryce ordered, and now Ledbetter seemed prepared to let him have his way. He made little sound as he walked towards the cage-like structure which contained the clock, and bent down: in a few moments he was back. "If anything goes wrong," he said, "some other clock will be the oldest. *That* one won't be there any longer."

Batten winced.

"Go on," Ledbetter ordered.

"I want to stick another of these little playthings up by the choir stalls," Bryce said. "It's easy as kiss your hand. One dab of Sticktite and it'll stay forever. Unless I use my remote control gadget. One squawk on the right wavelength, and upsadaisy!"

"You don't need —" Batten couldn't finish, it hurt him so much to speak.

"I know what we need," interrupted Bryce. "This is what I'm here for." He was obviously able to see more clearly now and turned into the nave. His footsteps echoed faintly as he went towards the altar, and the beam of his torch fell on the carved figures of saints and patriarchs about the pulpit.

Soon, the light fell on the wooden angels of the choir stalls, the coats of arms behind them.

Bryce made a scraping sound. There was a noise from outside; an aeroplane, high up. Bryce kicked against something and muttered an imprecation. Any sound was a blasphemy here and at this moment.

Batten said: "We can go that way."

"Don't try any tricks," Ledbetter ordered.

Soon, they caught up with Bryce as he came from the choir stalls, whistling softly under his breath. The sound was like a serpent's hiss. His face showed as the others approached.

"Which way?" he asked.

Batten said: "This way." He looked upwards at the great columns which supported the spire, always to him a source of wonder. Now, he was shaking and he felt very cold. If he ran, if he made the slightest attempt to stop them, he was sure Bryce would do what he had threatened. Yet here was his last chance to prevent this awful crime.

Here, he could break the contact by the simple pressing of a switch. It would take only a moment, and the first alarm would be silenced. And there were other switches. If he passed one, if he turned the key in this door without switching off, the whole cathedral would be filled with ringing clangour, and as he had told Ledbetter, first the Chief Security Officer would come, and almost as soon the close constable; in minutes, the police.

He had the power in his own hands.

Ledbetter could not stop him if he made the move.

But there was the 'bomb' in his own pocket. There were those now planted in the cathedral. So there was nothing at all he could do; he had waited too long, his fears had brought him to this state of utter helplessness.

"*Where?*" demanded Ledbetter.

"The — the door in front," Batten murmured, and he pressed the switch to make their path a safe one.

Oh, dear God, God forgive me. This is holy ground. There are the chapels where worshippers come, altars dedicated to the long dead saints; to St. Michael and St. Laurence and St. Margaret. Here the Lady Chapel which had survived Cromwell. Here, the shafts of Purbeck marble, here the effigy of William Longsword, bastard son of Henry II and his fair Rosamund; one like so many from this western land who had coerced King John to assent to Magna Carta. These things had great significance to him and he held them in awe. Forgive me, forgive me. He took his keys and by force of habit selected the one which would open the door leading to the cloisters, and also the steps which led up to the library. The door opened, very slowly; he had never known it so heavy. Or was that the weakness in his arms? There was no light beyond but the beam of the torch seemed brighter.

"*Where?*" Ledbetter demanded again.

"Up — up the stairs."

"*Stairs?*"

The beam wavered about and then fell on the narrow winding stone staircase which seemed to lead nowhere. It showed the cracks and the grooves made by countless feet on each tread; and the one stone wall. They stood at the foot for what seemed a long time, Bryce still whistling, *sss-sss-sss.*

"You go first, Bryce," Ledbetter said. "I'll come last."

"I — I must go first," Batten said. "I — I know where to switch off the contact."

"Watch this flicker," Bryce said.

"I'll watch him."

Batten went up a step at a time, Ledbetter almost on his heels. Then they reached the small landing and stood together in front of the ancient door. The light shone onto the panels and onto the keyhole. He touched another switch.

"That the library?" Ledbetter asked.

"Ye-yes."

"Make up your mind."

"Yes!"

"Open it," Bryce said, and dug him savagely in the ribs.

This was the last obstacle before the safe. In there, just beyond the door, were ancient books, manuscripts which were unique; records of the pious and the saintly and the noble; work of musicians and of artists and of scribes. And there, encased, secured, was the copy of Magna Carta. He could see the words as if they were written on the door:

THE SARUM

MAGNA CARTA

1215

Bryce kicked him.

"*Open it!*"

If he did, all would be lost.

But if he didn't, all would be lost, too. They could take the manuscript from here; they would soon find the right key. *There was nothing he could do.* He groped for and selected

11—TTOMC * *

the key, identifying it by touch. His shin ached; his ribs ached. He could kill these men! The beam shone on the keyhole and on his trembling fingers, and the key turned and Bryce shouldered him aside and pushed the door open.

There were the precious stores; the fabulous treasures; and at the end of the narrow crowded room, the greatest treasure of them all. And — and he had a key to that. He had been entrusted with a key lest he should come here and find a fire and need to save the charter. Now it showed beneath the heavy glass; and as all three of them drew closer, Bryce ahead and Batten next and Ledbetter breathing down his neck, even these two vandals seemed at last to be affected. For at least a minute none of them moved or spoke but looked down. There was a section, bright and clear in the light of the torch.

The torch trembled.

"Don't," Batten pleaded. "Don't — don't take it. Don't —"

"You bloody fool," Bryce said. "That's worth a million nicker. *Open it.*"

"Oh, God —"

"You snivelling basket, open it!"

Oh, dear God, dear God. It was happening and he was doing it: he was letting them take this priceless vellum. He, Thomas Batten, was betraying everything he had ever believed in.

Ledbetter opened the metal box. Inside there was velvet; dark red velvet; red, like blood. Ledbetter took a square of this out. Batten — *Batten* — unlocked and freed and lifted the relic he had never before touched, and placed it in the box. His own breathing was hardly audible; theirs was hushed.

"Let's go," Ledbetter said.

"Do we need to lock up?" asked Bryce.

"It will be out of the country before anybody knows it's gone."

Bryce gave a snorting, hissing laugh. Batten missed a step, but no one touched him now. Bryce led the way, shining his torch carefully. Batten moved between them. Ledbetter had the fireproof box clutched under his arm, and held the side of the narrow staircase with his free hand. They reached the bending columns and stood for a moment beneath the tower vault and walked, still breathless, along the nave and to the doors through which they had come, Bryce a yard ahead. He opened the door slowly and it squeaked. He stepped out gingerly, as if he expected the ground to collapse beneath him — and then he stood absolutely rigid, a hiss of breath like the slash of a knife.

Ledbetter called urgently: "What is it? What is it?"

"The bloody cops are everywhere," Bryce said. "They're even on the roofs."

* * *

Tom Batten's first thought was 'thank God'. But the feeling did not last. He had not the slightest doubt of the viciousness in Bryce and Ledbetter; it was as if they were primed to kill. They crept silently back into the cathedral and the door closed. Batten felt one man pull at his shoulder, the other at his coat. Both were breathing harshly.

He gasped: "I — I didn't bring them!"

"You're going to send them away," Ledbetter growled. Something in his voice told of his own fear. "You're going out to tell them that if they try to stop us, we'll press that switch, and there won't be anything left of their precious cathedral." There he was, holding the case, and Bryce was behind Batten, cold fingers gripping his neck. "Go and tell West what we've done," Ledbetter went on. "Don't forget a thing. The clock, the choir, the library — they will all go up in smoke if anyone tries to stop us getting away."

"And so will that whore up in the hills," Bryce said. "Get going. *Now*."

He opened the door and pushed Batten out, so that he was alone on the dark porch but able to see the cars beyond the walls, and the men standing, even two men on a roof, opposite.

He was gasping for breath.

He began to walk and then to shuffle and at last to run. He was halfway towards the nearest exit from where he stood before he remembered the bomb in his pocket. He took it out. He placed it carefully on the ground, then he began to run much faster and to cry out as he went.

"It's Batten! Tom Batten! Don't stop them, don't stop them!" He saw two men coming towards him and slowed down so that he could speak more clearly. "They've — they've got the Magna Carta! They'll blow it to pieces if you stop them. And — and — and oh God, they'll start fires all over the cathedral. Everywhere! You've got to let them go."

His breath caught when he stopped and he could not speak again; just gasped and struggled for breath.

He did not recognise West or Isherwood.

He did not realise how many were here: a tall dean whose work was mostly in the library, the one who had been addressing the coach party that afternoon. Two, three, four other clerics. Sir Richard Way, Chief Constable of the Police Region which included the Wiltshire Constabulary. Two women, one whose especial care was the library and who cherished the copy of Magna Carta at least as much as any child of her bosom.

And behind Batten the cathedral stood as solid and as stable now as in all its seven hundred years; within its walls explosive enough to cause so much damage that it would never be the same; might become a dark and smoking shell.

18

"Let Them Go"

BATTEN'S VOICE FADED into a gasping intake of breath, then
he began to breathe shallowly, as if he could not get the
air into his lungs. The first words which broke the silence
were from Kempton, who whispered: "Can't someone give
him a drink?" Two policemen moved forward. A man
behind the tall dean said quietly: "I'll take him to my
house."

Roger was aware of this, aware that Batten could not walk
without support and that the speaker and a policeman went
with him and he was aware of the tension in the men all
about him.

The tall dean asked in a bewildered way: "Can he really
mean it?"

"I think we ought to assume that he does," Roger said.

"What a dreadful dilemma, Dean Howe," another cleric
almost sobbed.

"Do you think there's a dilemma, sir?" Roger asked Sir
Richard Way.

Way was looking across at the mass of the cathedral; since
Batten had first appeared, he hadn't spoken. Would he always
be a shadowy figure, influencing rather than guiding his
men? Now he looked at Roger, and his ascetic face was
caught in a light from one of the nearby lamps; he was more
like a prelate than any of the clerics here.

"No," he answered. "We must let them go, of course."

A policeman, out of sight, muttered: "But we can't!"

A cleric, out of sight, said clearly: "Thank God, thank God!"

"Don't you agree, Superintendent?" asked Way in that thin and disapproving voice.

"Yes," Roger said briskly. "If I were senior officer here I would certainly let them get out of the cathedral."

"But they might get away with Magna Carta," a man said in a frightened voice.

"If we keep them in there they'll not only destroy the manuscript but almost certainly do untold damage to the building," Roger argued in an almost mechanical voice. "We simply haven't any choice, we must get them out of there peacefully."

"You mean, promise them safe passage and then pounce?"

"Five minutes must have passed already," Isherwood said gruffly. "We can't keep arguing much longer."

"I don't see how we can pounce if they have the manuscript," Roger replied to the Chief Constable. "They have to be allowed to get clear from the cathedral at least. Afterwards if we can pounce without risking damage to the manuscript —"

"Will you go and talk to them?"

"Yes."

The Chief Constable nodded.

"May I have Mr. Isherwood with me?" Roger asked.

"Yes. Of course."

"And if we have a floodlight turned on us they'll see there are only the two of us," Roger pointed out.

"I'll fix that, sir," a man by one of the cars said. "No problem."

"Then let's go."

Roger stepped between the white posts and for a moment seemed to be in complete darkness, for the branches of tall trees and the dark shape of a house intensified the shadows at this entrance. Before they had gone fifty yards, however, a light shone out from a car roof. At first only Isherwood was caught in the beam, which cast a strangely elongated shadow which soon included Roger's as they walked into the darkness. Roger had his amplifier in his left hand.

Lights showed at a dozen windows around the close.

Here and there the figures of men showed on the rooftops.

The footsteps of the two policemen sounded clearly on the macadam surface of the path. The brightness of the light behind them began to fade and the cathedral itself showed up more clearly, its grey stone reflecting some of the light. An aeroplane droned overhead, and seemed very loud. The two men marched in step, sleeves brushing now and again. They were already halfway to the doorway and neither had spoken.

At last, Isherwood said: "They couldn't have slipped out, could they?"

"They'll talk to us before they take any chance," Roger replied confidently. "We'll stop just outside the porch."

"Right."

Their footsteps made a rhythm. Left-right, left-right, left-right.

"When the bloody hell —" began Isherwood.

"That's far enough," a man called.

He was just beyond the porch. They could just see the outline of his face against the darkness of the wooden door and wooden panels at the far end. Both stopped as if commanded on the parade ground. Roger fought down an impulse to make a lunge towards the doorway.

"All right," he called. "We're here to talk."

"You're due to do what you're told if you want to save any of your precious junk," Ledbetter said. "Is that West?"

"Yes, I'm West. Chief Inspector Isherwood is with me."

"I don't care who's with you. West, I want clear passage, understand? If I don't get it —" The man was coming forward and a door creaked behind him and, ghostlike, another man appeared. "I'll press *this* little thing and the place will go up."

He held up a transistor control.

Roger had no doubt at all what it was; and no doubt at all that the man meant exactly what he said.

"I've got enough incendiary explosive to blow this rabbit hutch into little pieces," he said. "I just have to press a switch and there won't be any Magna Carta no mo'." Mockery was plain in his voice. "And when I press that switch it will set off an explosion beneath the high altar, so there won't be no altar no mo' either."

Isherwood growled: "You sacrilegious swine."

"Was that the poor Chief Inspector?" mocked Ledbetter. "Let me tell you something, Chief Inspector. This piece of old vellum means just one thing to me: money. A lot of money. But it won't get me a penny if I can't deliver it to my boss. As a piece of history to me it's a load of old junk. Don't talk to me about sacrilege, I don't go for religious hocus-pocus. Plain bloody superstition, that's all that is. Don't get me wrong. This goes with me or it goes up in smoke. And this is an electronic switch, I can press it now or a mile away, the result will be the same inside or outside the cathedral. Now, make up your mind. What's it to be?"

Roger asked: "Where is Linda Prell?"

"You'll find out when I'm clear away."

"No," Roger said. "I won't trade her."

"You've flicking well got to!" Ledbetter rasped.

"No," Roger said patiently, "I haven't got to. I don't have to let you go, I don't have to save the cathedral or Magna Carta. What I ought to do is jump you now; I might yet. Where's Linda Prell?"

There was a short pause and a rustle of movement before the other man appeared at Ledbetter's side and said in a loud whisper:

"Tell him. That bitch doesn't count any more."

Ledbetter said: "She's in a cave at a place called Hazebury Ring."

"Near Bodenham!" exclaimed Isherwood.

"So what?" Ledbetter sneered. "West, I tell you —"

Roger put the walkie-talkie to his lips and spoke very clearly. His voice did not travel far from this spot but it would reach every receiver and amplifier in the police cars and in the pockets of uniformed policemen. Another aircraft flew overhead and in the distance there was the louder noise of a small helicopter.

"This is Superintendent West calling Chief Constable Sir Richard Way and all officers surrounding the cathedral and other points assigned earlier this evening. The thieves with the copy of Magna Carta have an electronic device by which they can destroy the manuscript and do serious damage to the cathedral. They are about to leave the cathedral by the north door, and will proceed towards St. Anne's Gate, the postern of which is open. They must be allowed free passage to their car, and they must not be followed."

"*There's my boy!*" breathed Ledbetter.

"The car's a Ford Capri, metallic-blue in colour, just outside that gate," breathed the younger man with him.

"Their car is a metallic-blue Ford Capri," Roger repeated. He drew in a deep breath. "The two men are about to move out of the porch of the entrance. Any false step by any member of the force may lead to the destruction of —"

A woman, not far off, screamed: "Don't let them take it!"

A man cried: "Stop her!"

A searchlight swivelled from the top of a car towards a woman who was running from the wall where police cars were lined up. Two men ran in pursuit, others began to follow.

"*Don't let them, don't let them!*"

Roger said to Ledbetter: "I can answer for the police, I can't answer for the public. You'd better get moving."

Slowly, Ledbetter came out of the shadows of the porch into the pale searchlight beam. His accomplice moved with him. They looked at the running woman and the stream of men after her, almost catching up, then started towards the path which ran diagonally across the grass towards the St. Anne's Gate. Ledbetter muttered what sounded like "they'd better let us go," and quickened his pace. Roger heard a curious little grating sound from Isherwood and saw the man's jaws working; he was grinding his teeth. Roger gripped his arm and said: "Come on." He turned and strode towards the west gate. The woman was standing in a circle of men, still wailing her heart's protest, hysterical in distress.

Isherwood caught up with Roger.

"What's on your mind? The damage is done."

"Not yet," Roger said. "Not yet." He broke into a run and reached the police cars. "I want a local driver," he called. "Quick!"

A man standing by an empty car said: "Here, sir."

"Get out by that other gate, get us beyond Bodenham fast," Roger said. "Do you know Newall Lodge?"

"*I* do!" growled Isherwood, getting in.

"Yes, sir!" The local policeman was sliding behind the steering wheel.

"Take us to a point where we can approach it from the other direction," Roger ordered. "The Bournemouth road, isn't it?" He squeezed into a corner of the small car. "Jack, I've just realised what I saw on the lawn of Withers's house — marks made by a helicopter on landing. He blamed a grass-cutting machine, he was so anxious to explain them away, but they were caused by landing bars."

"My God!" breathed Isherwood.

"Add that to the chalk on his drive and there's not much doubt that a car which had been on that chalk came here. There's no chalk anywhere near here, but there was plenty at Basingstoke. And if I remember there's a thick copse at the back of his lawn surrounded by a four- or five-foot fence."

"There is," Isherwood growled.

"Tall enough to hide a small helicopter if the blade was removed," Roger said. "Is there a radio here, driver?"

"Yes, sir!" The man unhooked one from the dashboard and handed it over the back seat. Roger took it and switched on. "This is Superintendent West calling all officers in or near Bodenham. Proceed from Bodenham to Hazebury Ring and search for a cave in which Police Officer Prell is reported to be captive. Repeat. This is —" He repeated the message, and immediately replies came: "Message received," from half-a-dozen different points. Roger leaned forward and put the telephone back, as Isherwood growled:

"I don't get it."

"If they're going to Newall Lodge you can be sure they have a receiving set with our wavelength," Roger said. "So now they'll know that the cordon's on its way." They were through the gate and on a roundabout; some distance along one road which fed the roundabout was St. Anne's Gate, and Ledbetter must have reached the gate by now. He peered out of his window, Isherwood out of the back; no car was approaching, no one appeared beneath the yellow street lights.

The driver was hurtling the car forward, turned left, went furiously along a winding road and then onto a dual carriageway which Roger had forgotten. On the left was the narrow road leading to the Lodge. A light glowed at the end of the drive, another near the house itself. Lights were on at the top of the house. The car flashed past the other end of the road which debouched into the dual carriageway, and the driver began to slow down.

"Want me to drive close, sir?"

"No. Park here and we'll walk. Don't slam doors."

"Right," the driver said. He pulled off the road just beyond the dual carriageway and before the engine stopped, the doors were opening. "This way," the driver said. "There's a path leading to a cottage and a narrow one to the fence and the front of the house." He led the way as if he were a born poacher. Two or three cars passed, throwing their headlights eerily through wooded land and hedges and reflecting from the windows of Newall Lodge.

"Look!" the driver whispered, and spread his arms to stop the other two.

They could see beyond the tennis court and the fence to the house itself. There, quite unmistakable, were the skeletal outlines of a small helicopter. It was being pushed on to the lawn itself, and they could just make out a wheeled base on which it stood. The stars gave constant light, the headlamps brighter moments. Two men were pushing the machine, but neither was visible enough to be identifiable.

"Closer," breathed Roger.

"What are you planning to do?" demanded Isherwood, hoarsely.

"By the time Ledbetter gets here he'll be too far from the cathedral to do any damage there and everyone here will think they're safe. They'll want to be as careful with Magna Carta as we would be. So we simply close in."

"All *three* of us," Isherwood said sardonically. "They'll be armed."

"Jack," Roger said, "all we have to do is keep that manuscript safe. I'd have sent for military helicopters if I hadn't felt sure the thieves had our wavelength. I think we three can pull it off. They won't be expecting us from here.

One of us needs to grab that package and run hell-for-leather for cover — there's plenty of cover about." He waved to the small thickets of trees and bushes. "The moment we've got it we can call for help, we won't be on our own for long." When Isherwood didn't answer, Roger went on: "Will you go for the manuscript, or shall I?"

"I will," Isherwood muttered.

"Sir," the driver said, "I've got a better idea — I think."

"Let's have it." Roger spun round on him. "What is it?"

"There are ten or so flats in the stables, mostly occupied by youngish people. And I know for a fact that some of them have shotguns and rifles — lot of pigeon shooting around here. I could nip round and rouse them. Linda Prell's brother-in-law would jump at the chance."

"Get moving!" Roger urged.

The driver went off with skilful quiet; there was hardly a rustle of movement. The two men had the helicopter in position on a stretch of grass about a hundred yards from the house itself. It stood on a flat trolley-like platform which had small wheels. As his eyes grew more accustomed to the dark, Roger saw one of the men climb up into the bulbous cockpit of the machine; the other stayed on the land.

Lights began to play among the trees. Roger and Isherwood turned towards the dual carriageway leading from Salisbury, whence the headlights came. An indicator began to flicker and the car swung towards the village, coming very fast. The headlights swayed. The engine began to hum. The car turned into the driveway of Newall Lodge until its lights shone on the red brick of the house and reflected on all the windows — and for a split second shone onto the silvery head of John Withers. Next moment the light was switched off and when the car itself appeared only its parking lights showed. The tyres grated on the gravel and took a path which ran right round the big lawn, and seemed to head straight for Roger and Isherwood.

The car stopped, cutting the helicopter off from the crouching policemen. Doors opened, and three, not two, men sprang out; Stephenson was here and could only have been picked up on the road between here and Salisbury. He must have driven like a demon. For a moment Ledbetter and he were within twenty yards of Roger.

Ledbetter carried the square package.

He turned towards the men on the grass, holding his prize high. He had both hands on it, so could not be holding the detonator switch. He rounded the car, calling in a quiet voice which nevertheless carried back to Roger as well as forward to Withers and the other man, who climbed down from the machine.

"Here it is," he gloated. "The one and only." He paused. "Now hand over the money."

"And hand it over fast," the younger man said roughly. "If you don't —"

"He'll hand over the money," Stephenson said. "I know too much about him for him to doublecross me."

A car came whining along the highway, drowning his words. Roger strained his ears but heard only snatches of the voices. He did not hear the menace in the young man's voice.

"... *don't hand over, your bloody house and everything in it will go up in smoke. You think I trusted you? Not on your life!*"

Nor did Roger hear Withers say:

"*I know. I found where you wired it — to the central-heating time switch.*"

Roger heard the youth laugh. *Laugh.*

Withers said so that Roger could hear: "I know how much you know, Neil, and I'm beginning to find out how much you talk."

Next moment there was a sharp crack of sound: a shot. It seemed to echo and re-echo, like a sigh. *Ack-ack-ack-aack-aaack.* Another followed, just as sharp, following a gasp from closer to the car. Ledbetter's head and shoulders disappeared beneath the car. The young man began to cry:

"Don't shoot. Don't —"

"*Ack!*"

Ack-ack-ack-aack-aaack-aaaack, the second shot sighed as the young man fell out of sight.

"You can't —" began Stephenson, but a third shot cracked and slowly its echoes gradually faded into silence. Stephenson did not even cry out.

19

The Killer

ISHERWOOD SAID SOMETHING under his breath: it sounded like: "He's killed all three." The silence was broken by the man from the helicopter, who said clearly: "They might be foxing." The two men by the helicopter moved forward, and then also vanished from sight, obviously bending over Ledbetter and his accomplices. An owl called. A dog barked.

Roger and Isherwood began to crawl forward, fearful of making too much sound. A car came humming along the dual carriageway, drowning their movements so that they could hurry, but they kept behind the car for cover. They broke through the bushes and were on to grass when Withers said:

"So we've got it."

"Now I've got to get away with it," the other man said in a voice Roger could not possibly mistake.

It was Caldicott's. *Caldicott's.*

"Yes," Withers said. It was difficult to understand the tone in his voice as he went on: "We can wait ten minutes."

"We can't wait two!"

"Frank," said Withers, "I want to see it."

"You can see it in New York," Caldicott rasped. "Don't play the fool now. I've had enough trouble shaking off the police. I don't want any more. Give it to me."

Caldicott.

He must have come straight here from Lords, and had managed to leave London without anyone suspecting where he was heading. Caldicott with his broad smile and rubbery lips and rugged blood-hound face. Roger could picture him sitting in the kitchen only that morning.

"John," Caldicott urged. "Minutes might count."

"You heard West call his dogs off."

"I wouldn't trust West not to pull a fast one."

"The cars moved away, and the police scattered," Withers said reassuringly. "There's no danger, Frank. I only want —"

He broke off.

Roger reached the car at one end and Isherwood the other. So far they had been hidden by the car and neither man could have been seen. This was the moment of acute danger. Roger saw the two men facing each other, with the bodies of the other three only a few feet away. Neither Withers nor Caldicott was facing the car, but were broadside-on. Withers had the packet in his arms. In fact he was hugging it to him under his left arm and keeping it in position with his right; there was enough light to show the gun in his right hand. It was even light enough to see the way the eyes of each man glinted.

There was more.

A man appeared on the far side of the house, clear against the sky. Another appeared from a tree on the far side of the grass. Both held guns; they were not near enough to be identified as rifles but each was held as a soldier would hold one, and each man was crouching, and moving slowly. A third appeared in silhouette against a bush smothered in white blossom.

"For God's sake!" Caldicott rasped. "We've risked our necks for this! Let me have it, *now*."

That was the moment when Roger sprang forward. On the same instant, Isherwood leapt, and from the men on the far side of the grounds there came two rifle shots, while the men from Stables House came racing. Withers and Caldicott seemed to spring apart, Withers still hugging the package and flinging his gun arm forward. If he fired at point-blank range how could he miss?

Roger flung himself forward.

Withers fired. *Ack-ack-ack-ack*.

The bullet cut through the padding of the shoulder of Roger's jacket and grazed the skin, but the pain was so slight he hardly noticed it. Arms outstretched to their limit, he clutched at Withers's ankles, missed with his right, gripped with his left, and pulled. Withers went staggering. Roger could only see his feet and legs, knew he was falling, feared for the package. Withers made a crabwise movement to try to save himself, but failed, but the package fell on him instead of him falling on the package. Two men including the driver of the police car reached Withers and the policeman bundled onto him and then knelt astride, forcing his gun-hand open. The gun dropped. Roger rolled over and got to his knees as a man touched him and asked:

"Are you all right, sir? Are you all right?"

"Fine," grunted Roger. "Fine." He saw Isherwood standing with that precious package, clutching it to him with both arms but as gently as he would hold a baby. More men came running; some women, too. Caldicott was standing between two men without attemping to escape; and there was a sharp click as the driver handcuffed Withers to him. Caldicott called out in a muffled voice: "Well, I didn't know he was going to shoot the others. I just didn't know. You can't charge me with murder."

"You didn't object, either," Roger said coldly. "Jack," he said to Isherwood, "we must report this at once."

"I've reported, sir," the driver of the police car said, shrill-voiced. "I used my walkie-talkie. They should be out here in a few moments."

While some of the men and women from the flats were asking what was going on, while Withers and Caldicott were being taken to Newall Lodge, both handcuffed to police officers, cars began to stream from Salisbury along the dual carriageway, headlights thrusting great beams; and one after the other swung into the drive of Newall Lodge. In the first car came the Chief Constable and tall Dean Howe. Others spilled out of their cars, among them Childs, and his photographer. Isherwood held the precious package towards the dean who stretched out both arms for it. The long-haired photographer's camera did not stop flashing. Withers made no attempt to turn his face away but Caldicott turned his this way and that to avoid the camera.

Withers said harshly: "You'll regret this night's work, West. Don't you ever forget it."

Roger made no comment, in fact hardly noticed the threat. There was much to do and much more to think about and his head was near-splitting.

Out of the confusion grew a kind of order.

Roger charged Withers with murder and Caldicott with receiving goods knowing them to be stolen. Even as he used the words he wondered how trite one could sound. Both men were taken off in police cars. An elderly man and woman, house-servants at the Lodge, were scared but helpful. They took Roger and Isherwood, Kempton and another Salisbury man over the house. Every wall was covered with pictures, the house itself was a treasure chest.

Roger went into a cloakroom and dowsed his face in cold water; it helped his head a little. He even turned on the hot water tap to wash his hands. The central-heating boiler in the cellar was almost directly beneath the spot where he stood.

"We can't really go through the contents here tonight," Roger said, when he went out, "and I'm too tired to do anything else properly. Can we put the house under close guard, sir, and get cracking in the morning?"

"Yes," the Chief Constable said. "You've done a lot more than your share."

"Share," the Dean choked. "Share! I don't know how anyone will ever be able to thank you, Mr. West. I really don't know."

He both sounded and looked like a man from whom a great burden had been lifted.

"Shall I drive you?" Kempton asked Roger.

"One of us ought to stay here," Roger said. "I'm not even sure I'm right to leave anything until morning."

He was standing in the hall of Newall Lodge, with the whole dark night beyond him when he saw lights. Not one or two but a dozen at least on the hill opposite the house, a mile or more away. That was the moment when he remembered Linda Prell; when he realised that he had completely forgotten her. The others turned and stared and it

12—TTOMC * *

seemed that all had forgotten too, and there was silence everywhere.

The radio telephone of a car crackled. A man leaned inside and snatched up the receiver. Squawks and squeaks came through and then the man raised his voice and shouted:

"They've found her. She's safe! They want an ambulance, but she's safe!"

*   *   *

"Alan," Roger West said to Kempton, "I'd like to go and tell Batten." He glanced at Isherwood. "If you don't mind."

"Of course not," Isherwood said. "I know what house he's in at the close. I'll come with you."

"I wish you'd stay here," Roger said. "This house needs a careful watch and someone ought to go through it from attic to basement. Ledbetter talked about a bomb attached to the central-heating plant, and it had better be checked."

Isherwood seemed eager for the chance.

"I'll get cracking right away," he said. Then added hurriedly to Kempton: "With you, Alan! And I'll get someone to drive you into town, Handsome. My God, what a night. But thank God we've saved it."

*   *   *

Batten, sitting in an easy chair, saw Roger come into the room and began to struggle to his feet. Roger waved him down. It was a small room with several armchairs and a baby grand piano adorned with family portraits including one of the man who had brought Batten here. The anxiety on Batten's face seemed to have aged him many years, but it began to ease when he saw Roger's expression.

"She's safe," Roger told him immediately. "So is the manuscript, Tom, and we've got the two ringleaders." He moved across to Batten's side and touched his arm; that movement was the first to cause a slight pain in his shoulder, bringing the first realisation that he had been hurt. "The rest will sort itself out."

"I know," Batten said. "Gosh, I'm thankful!"

"Did you hear anything from either of the men which we ought to know?" asked Roger.

"No, sir, I can't say I did. But I'll tell you one thing, though. That young chap, he was a whiz at explosives and remote control. He fixed up the gadget in the library and behind the altar in no time. And take it from me, sir, they would have burned the cathedral and the Magna Carta without any compunction."

"I'm quite sure you're right," Roger said.

The words were hardly out of his mouth when there was a sound of a car drawing up outside. Batten stared past Roger towards the window. The light shone from the room to show a car door opening and a big, heavy woman climbing out, awkwardly. It flashed across Roger's mind that this was Batten's wife, and the expression on Batten's face told him his guess was right.

A woman at the outside door spoke in a broad Wiltshire accent.

"Is my Tom all right, then? Doctor, will you tell me — is my Tom all right?"

"He's fine, Mrs. Batten," said the man who had brought Batten here. "He needs rest, a good night's sleep will make all the difference to him."

"Is he all right?" the woman asked, as if she had not heard a word. "That's all I want to know."

She went into the room as Roger went out. She had a big, broad, weathered face and beautiful blue eyes and an enormous bosom, and he had never seen any human being broader across the hips. She disappeared, making a gusty sound, and then cried out as if in exultation.

"Tom! Oh Tom, they told me you'd been hurt. Tom, love, don't worry, I'll look after you, don't 'ee worry about a thing."

*　　　*　　　*

It was after three o'clock that morning before Roger got into bed.

He was physically tired out, and wondered if Batten could be any more exhausted than he. He was elated because of the triumph and still shocked by the cold-blooded way in which Withers had killed the three men who had worked with and for him. He was anxious for news about Stephenson's 'wife', and was anxious to sleep for a few hours and then go and search Newall Lodge, but most of all he was anxious to talk to Linda Prell, to find out what she had overheard.

The plot to steal the copy of Magna Carta, presumably.

Or could it have been something else? Was there still more to this affair?

20

Kempton's Day

ISHERWOOD WAS ONE of eight men at Newall Lodge. He went into every room and looked into every cupboard with Kempton. Other men walked the grounds, and double-checked everything. The time clock in the cellar, by the side of the hot-water boiler, ticked away all the time. Neither man took any notice. There were three rooms in the cellar and all were filled with old paintings, prints and frames. In one corner there were some turpentine and turps substitute, and a bench on which paintings were cleaned, or where corners or slips were tested, to check age.

Isherwood yawned.

"Ever seen anything like this?" he asked Kempton.

"I know what it reminds me of," Kempton said. "A fence's store."

"Fence?"

"It looks as if Withers is always in the market for stolen pictures, holds them until they're cool, and then sells them somewhere out of England," Kempton hazarded. "He had the perfect set-up. This helicopter lark isn't new. I wouldn't mind betting we'll get a lot of surprises in the morning. I wouldn't mind starting now, and have a surprise packet ready for Handsome."

"Count me out," Isherwood said.

"I'm not serious," Kempton admitted. He did not add that above everything else he wanted to do something which would impress Handsome West deeply. The feeling that he hadn't impressed West had grown stronger; he suspected that he had been left here as a kind of sop to his pride.

A man came hurrying down the stairs and along the passage towards them; it was the little man who had driven Roger and Isherwood here. He looked excited, bright eyes shining, as he approached.

"Bath have picked up Mrs. Stephenson!" he announced with deep satisfaction. "Now we've got the whole bunch." He looked about the room and the mass of pictures, and then glanced at the time clock which was ticking away. He started, in alarm, and stepped forward, saying as if to himself: "What the hell's that?" Then he turned round and went on: "Sorry, sir. But that's fresh wiring there — that thin wire." He went closer to the clock, taking out his glasses and peering short-sightedly. "You know what *that* is, don't you?" he asked in a tense voice. "That's a bomb set to go off when the water-heater starts up in the morning."

"But Withers said he'd found the wiring," Isherwood protested. "I thought —"

"Fact is there's a charge of nitro inside the face of the clock, I can see it," said the little man. "Maybe they wired it twice for safety. But if we stop the clock ticking away we'll be okay." He peered more closely and then went on in a choky voice: "It's set to go off about *now*." He pulled at the glass cover of the clock but could not pull it off, so he touched a switch at one side.

The ticking stopped; the following silence seemed unearthly.

"I — I'll hold it while you go, gents," the small man said.

"Get the house cleared of people, Jack," Kempton ordered. "I'll keep my finger on that switch — just get the place cleared, and call the fire brigade."

"It might — it *might* go off," the driver insisted. "I'm afraid if I switch off the clock it will blow, this just holds it."

"Then the quicker you get some firemen here the better," retorted Kempton, placing his finger over the little man's, who slid his away. He pressed, lightly. The clock did not tick. "Hurry!" he urged Isherwood, who moved quickly away and up the stairs. His voice boomed out, giving instructions. Kempton stood as relaxed as he could be, his finger quite steady. Footsteps sounded overhead, then faded. Kempton looked at the framed and the unframed paintings, wondering whether he was right about Withers. He did not know how long he had been there when the footsteps of two men sounded, and in a few moments the little driver and a man in army uniform came hurrying.

"Bit of luck, sir," the driver said. "We've an R.A.O.C. unit at Salisbury, they were called to the cathedral in case of emergency and came on here. You can leave it to the expert now, sir."

A few minutes later the expert reported: "You had two or three minutes to spare, Inspector. Plenty of time."

Kempton burst out laughing. Isherwood threw up his hands. The little driver grinned as he followed them out of the house and into the grounds as more of the bomb disposal men moved in.

"They'll go over the place with a fine tooth comb," Kempton remarked. "I don't think I'll wake Handsome, unless you particularly want to."

"All I want to do," said Isherwood, "is sleep."

*　　　*　　　*

The girl in black-and-white cap and apron who woke Roger with his morning tea was neither pert nor pretty, but obviously she was in awe of him. His eyes were heavy and his mouth tacky, but it was after nine, past time he was up. Yet he spent minutes at the window, looking out on the cathedral spire. Next he glanced through the newspapers, all of which carried old news of the Salisbury case; Magna Carta wasn't even mentioned! He had a quick bath and shower and was having bacon and eggs in the room when his telephone bell rang. He was positioned so as to reach it without getting up. He finished a succulent mouthful and said: "West."

"Good morning, sir." It was a brisk Kempton. "I asked the hotel to call me as soon as you were up. Did you have a good night?" There was a trace of smugness in Kempton's voice; as well as the Cockney overtones there was positively a purr.

"Very," Roger said. "Where are you?"

"Newall Lodge, sir."

"I'll be there in twenty minutes. Was Mrs. Stephenson charged with conspiracy?"

"She hasn't been charged but she's coming in to answer questions."

"Fair enough," Roger said. "Was anything found in Stephenson's room at Bath?"

"He had three canvasses in a false bottom of his suitcase and one of our Bath chaps recognised one as having been stolen from Lord Levers a year ago," Kempton answered.

"Well, we shouldn't be surprised."

"No, sir."

After a pause, Roger asked: "How is Linda Prell?"

"*Much* better, according to her doctor," Kempton replied. "She will be able to make a report this morning. She'll be going to her sister's so we can see her at Newall Lodge, too."

"Good. Batten?"

"He's here," Kempton said. "He ignored the doctor's advice and reported for duty."

"Then I'll see him there, too," Roger said with satisfaction. "How long have you been at the house?"

"Since half-past six," Kempton answered. "I couldn't get to sleep so I decided to make a straight run through here." The purring note of deep satisfaction was very much more clear.

Roger did not wait to find out why, but rang off and finished his breakfast, acutely aware of the one he had had with Caldicott. He had seldom met a more likeable man. It was Linda Prell and Batten who were on his mind when he reached his car in the car park. Ten minutes later he turned into the drive of Newall Lodge, passed two policemen and a crowd of thirty or forty people, went slowly up the drive and was immediately aware of Childs of the *Herald* and his long-haired photographer. Roger nodded but didn't pause as he passed more policemen just outside and two in the big hall itself.

Kempton came hurrying from the door which led to the cellar; and for a sober, even phlegmatic man he looked eager and excited. His eyes were red-rimmed from lack of sleep.

"Good morning, sir," he said briskly. "I wonder if you could come into the cellar first?"

"If you like," Roger said, knowing there must be a very good reason.

He guessed that Kempton had made a discovery of great importance but he was not even slightly prepared for what he saw when the Chief Inspector stood aside for him to enter the main room. Last night, this had been a fair-sized room, fifteen feet by twenty, perhaps, but now the 'wall' at the far end had been opened to show another gallery beyond; and as he walked past row upon row of pictures, mostly unframed but for protective wooden slats, he saw at least two more galleries.

"I've already identified a Picasso, a Monet, two El Grecos, a Holbein and I *think* some Michelangelo cartoons. This is a storehouse of stolen paintings, sir! I'd say two million pounds' worth at least. And — just wait a moment." He sounded like an elated schoolboy as he pushed past Roger to the cement-faced wall which really seemed to be the end. He pressed a button and the wall opened to show a flight of stone steps which led upwards; pressed another button and daylight shone on to the well of the staircase. "Go ahead, sir," he urged. "You'll come out to the spot where they kept the helicopter, behind a wooden fence."

Roger climbed the easy-to-mount steps until his head and shoulders were above ground. All about him was grass and trees and shrubs. When he stood up, he saw that the fence had been moved and Newall Lodge stood in the sunlight, its weathered red brick and the vines about its walls looking so peaceful.

As he stood there, a car pulled up outside the house and for the first time he set eyes on Linda Prell.

From the porch, Tom Batten moved forward.

Roger was near enough to see how she and Batten moved towards each other; and how they checked themselves. He saw Isherwood come out of the house and speak to the girl. She *was* little more than a girl; pale-faced, tired-looking, but with attractive hair and a nice, homely face; and a good but comparatively slim figure. Roger quickened his pace, with Kempton hurrying behind him. He hoped Isherwood wouldn't

question her before he arrived. No: Isherwood looked
towards him and mentioned the house, then led the girl in.
When Roger arrived she was sitting in a Regency armchair
in the book-lined room where Roger had talked to John
Withers. Kempton and Tom Batten followed him in.

"Miss Prell," Isherwood said, "this is Superintendent West
of New Scotland Yard — and Chief Inspector Kempton,"
he added belatedly.

At closer quarters, Roger saw the clearness of the girl's
grey eyes, and the straightness of her gaze. He motioned to
her not to get up, shook hands, and smiled as much at Isherwood as at Linda Prell.

"It may seem an anticlimax to you," he said, "but all of
us are agog to hear what you overheard to make them
abduct you."

Isherwood could not restrain himself.

"*Did* they talk about stealing Magna Carta?" he demanded.
"Was that it?"

"No," she answered quietly. "They did talk of a big
deal, and said the goods would be too hot to keep locally.
I was by the window, I'd gone to try to hear what Stephenson
was talking about so secretly. I suppose I shouldn't have, but
they went out to the bar, it seemed a golden opportunity
for me to get in. They came back into the room almost at
once, and started to talk." Linda Prell paused for breath;
the first real indication of weakness, but she soon went on:
"They started talking about releasing stolen paintings, even
arguing about how long it took for them to get cool, I was
appalled." She stopped again, and looked beyond Roger
towards the door, where Batten hovered.

"Don't hurry," Roger said.

Linda Prell looked back at him.

"Thank you," she said. "But I'm all right, really. It —
it's a bit overwhelming to have *you* questioning me, sir!"
She managed to smile, Roger to chuckle. "That's really all
the facts, sir," she went on, "but I sensed there was something else, and since I've had time to think back I'm nearly
certain they knew I was there, and didn't talk about the
main subject. That may just be hindsight, of course. They
must have known I was there, that's why the man Ledbetter

attacked me — Ledbetter and Bryce. They made me get into their car . . ."

"I can understand what happened," Roger said. "I'm not going to question you too much now, but there's one question I want you to think about very carefully. Did either of the men mention a man called Nicodemus?"

Linda's eyes widened, obviously in surprise. Roger felt suddenly quite sure that the name meant something to her.

"Yes," she replied. "Stephenson said something about the big deal being able to make or break even Nicodemus, and they both laughed. And the two men who held me prisoner sometimes talked about someone they called Old Nick."

"So they laughed when they talked about Nicodemus," Roger mused, "and the other two talked about Old Nick." He pondered for a few moments and then went on: "Once we know who he is we'll really know everything. Meanwhile, if it hadn't been for the chance you took the Sarum Magna Carta would be on its way to the United States by now. I don't suppose anyone will ever thank you — unless Tom Batten finds a way," he added, smiling, and Batten came slowly towards her.

It was as if to this couple there were no other people in the world, yet not far away, in her cottage, was Batten's wife. In a flash thought Roger wondered how they would work out their lives, then his thoughts switched to Nicodemus. "They both laughed," Linda had said. Old Nick was the biggest fence in paintings and works of art in the United States. Fence; buyer of stolen goods. There could hardly be a bigger fence in stolen works of art than John Withers. Only a man who operated on a massive scale could keep so much in stock; and only a man with all the self-confidence in the world would dare to keep the hoard here and release pieces a few at a time.

Goodison had talked of Nicodemus being a man *or a group of men.*

Could John Withers be the British side of 'Nicodemus'? Had there been an offer from the American side for Magna Carta thus sparking off the whole deal? Had Stephenson and

Ledbetter known his identity? Was that why they had been killed so ruthlessly, to make sure they couldn't talk?

Who would know?

Withers would deny it whether it was the truth or not, but Caldicott had been in at the kill. He couldn't talk to Caldicott soon enough.

*   *   *

The man was still in his cell, awaiting a hearing at the magistrates' court later in the day. He looked as lugubrious as ever and there was even a smile in his eyes when he said:

"Sorry I can't offer you breakfast, Superintendent."

"I'm in need of much more than breakfast," Roger replied. "You know you'll go down for a very long time, don't you?"

"You're not a man to rub anything in without a good reason," remarked Caldicott. "What are you offering me? Kid gloves treatment if I tell you everything I know?"

"And almost certainly a much lighter sentence if you turn Queen's evidence," Roger said.

"To tell you the truth I've been thinking a lot about that," replied Caldicott, "and I think I'll do a deal. I used to be a very happy runner who made a comfortable living without a lot of work, but Withers discovered my judgment was exceptional and he needed someone much better than he had. So I went in with him. He's one of a syndicate of fences who will buy really big for customers who don't mind if their treasures have been stolen. He and his American associates must know more millionaires than I know people! He planned Magna Carta without my knowing, though — at first, that is. Then we heard of the preview and the sale at Leech's, that seemed the golden opportunity. Explain our — that is Stephenson's and my presence — by the pictures while the major job was being pulled. It would have worked, too, if it hadn't been for that policewoman."

"It might have worked," Roger conceded. "Do you know why Withers killed Stephenson?"

"Two reasons," Caldicott replied. "The first was that Stephenson was asking for too big a share, but the strongest reason was that Stephenson told his Sarah, and Sarah told me! From that moment on Stephenson stopped being reliable. If she'd been his wife it might not have mattered but he changes his sleeping partners every few months, and this meant he was getting to the stage when he had to boast. He let Sarah think it was his idea, but . . ."

There were a great many more details but none of them was of vital significance, until Roger asked:

"Do you know Withers's associates in New York?"

"No. But I shouldn't think they would be too hard to find once you started tracing his movements over there. He visits New York at least once a year." Caldicott gave a wry smile, and went on: "Do what you can for me, Handsome, won't you? I'm going to miss cricket like hell!"

"I'll do what I can," promised Roger, and he went out.

A few minutes later he was talking to Goodison in New York and he had never heard a more excited man.

"That's the greatest news I ever had as a policeman," he cried. "Oh, boy, I can't wait to get busy. What's he like? How much stuff was he hoarding? . . . All right, all right, I'll wait for an official report later, and let you know the moment I've any news. If you can let me know the approximate dates he's been in New York . . . Thanks for calling."

*　　　*　　　*

Every newspaper carried the story, most used nothing else on the front page. Janet West telephoned to say how wonderful it was. Richard, their younger son, cabled from Malawi where he was making a film: "Didn't expect my father to become a national hero." Martin, their elder son, was waiting when Roger reached home.

"I couldn't bear to think of you cooking your own dinner tonight, Dad," he said. "It's mixed grill. Two sausages, or three?"

*　　　*　　　*

"I knew that he was interested in paintings, and I knew he planned a big deal in Salisbury," Sarah 'Stephenson' said. "But I knew no details and had no part in it. I hope you will believe that. And I hope you won't need me to give evidence, Mr. West. I am practically penniless in England."

"I doubt if we shall need more than your signed statement," Roger said.

"I hope very much that you won't." Her voice sounded and her expression was aloof, but both warmed suddenly, and she stammered unexpectedly, and then asked in a voice that was scarcely audible: "May I see Frank Caldicott? I can't claim to be an old friend, we only met last week, but —" She broke off.

"I see no reason why not," Roger said. "They will all be remanded in custody for a week, but there's no reason why they shouldn't have visitors."

"They," she echoed, and closed her eyes. "Yes. Yes, of course. But please not all at one time."

*   *   *

"No objection at all," Isherwood said, and then added with a rush: "No chance of her slipping him a dram of poison, I suppose?"

"You could always have her searched if you're worried," Roger said drily.

*   *   *

Coppell sat at his desk and listened, broke in with an occasional question, placed his big fingers on his desk, and began to smile. There was always a semi-sneer about his smile, but it was a physical thing, not born of mood.

"Well, some would say you had the luck of the devil, even if Old Nick didn't! Anyhow, Handsome, bloody good job. It won't do you any harm in the other business, either. You should get some official news about that before too long. They wanted to give you precise terms of reference, and I suggested you might be able to help with that!" He was highly amused at his own temerity but the amusement soon faded. "How did you find Kempton? He's in line for promotion."

"You won't find a better man on his day," Roger answered, "or a steadier one any time."

"Good," Coppell said. "Thanks. Well, you'll tidy things up with Salisbury, won't you?"

*   *   *

"The truth is I don't know how things will work out for Linda Prell and Batten," Jack Isherwood said. "I don't think he could bring himself to divorce his wife. She must know how things are and will go along with the situation — if he doesn't break up the home, she won't break up his *affaire*. Don't ask me how long it will last like that, though."

"I'll always be interested to hear," Roger told him.

"And I'll always pass on anything I learn," Isherwood replied. "Handsome, there's one thing I don't think I've ever told you."

"What's that?" asked Roger.

"What a treat it has been working with you," answered Isherwood.

Roger put down the receiver a few minutes afterwards, and turned to the letters on his desk. There was one, unopened, wih the words *Diocese of Salisbury* on the envelope, which was addressed in a beautiful hand. He opened it, and read:

Dear Mr. West,

There is no way of thanking you. But we shall all try. We hope — we hope fervently — that you can come to Salisbury two weeks from today, when there will be a special service of thanksgiving for this new salvation.

Yours most sincerely . . .

It was signed by the tall Dean Howe.